THE
WAGES OF SIN

MATT BRAUN

St. Martin's Paperbacks

THE WAGES OF SIN

Copyright © 1984 by Avon Books.

For information address St. Martin's Press, 175 Fifth Avenue, New York, NY 10010.

ISBN: 978-0-312-99786-1

Our books may be purchased in bulk for promotional, educational, or business use. Please contact your local bookseller or the Macmillan Corporate and Premium Sales Department at 1-800-221-7945, ext. 5442, or by e-mail at MacmillanSpecialMarkets@macmillan.com.

Printed in the United States of America

Avon Books edition / May 1984
St. Martin's Paperbacks edition / November 2004

St. Martin's Paperbacks are published by St. Martin's Press, 175 Fifth Avenue, New York, NY 10010.

10 9 8 7 6 5 4 3 2

THE
WAGES OF SIN

ONE

Four armed men rode the worn, dusty trail along
Sandies Creek. Though it was dark, the land was
still hot from the August sun, which had driven the
temperature to a hundred and two in the shade during
the day. The clear sky, sounds of water burbling, the
peaceful rhythmic noise made by the steady trot of
the horses, and the bright half-moon made a setting
for romance, not for cold-blooded murder.

The three riders moved with determination behind
their leader, jabbering about their Civil War exploits
or some recent drinking bout. Before the evening was
over, each would have two twenty-dollar gold pieces,
enough to keep them in popskull whiskey and fifty-
cent whores for a week at the outside. And for that
they were about to trade a life.

The man who had lured them out on the forty-
dollar mission smiled inwardly as he listened to the

three drifters. It never ceased to surprise him how easy it was in Reconstruction Texas to line up a few hardcases who'd do anything for a few dollars or to get back at a Yankee. During the War, they'd gone off to maintain the honor of the South and returned to dead and broken families, burnt-out farmhouses, and the corrupt and vicious occupation government. It was a festering sore that still burned in their hearts.

"Buck!" one of the riders shouted at him. He almost failed to answer since he'd made up the name only three days before.

"Buck!"

"Yeah," he finally responded.

"How much farther?"

"I figure two or three more miles. House is right where Sandies Creek flows into the Guadalupe."

That satisfied the grubby rider and he went back to jawing with his two sidekicks. Buck had told them that their target was a Yankee sympathizer who had turned his back on the South by selling cattle to the Union Army during the War. He'd lied, and the thought of it caused him to chuckle out loud.

Pitkin Taylor sat down to a late Sunday evening supper, a proud but troubled man. His son, Jim, sat at the other end of the rectangular table and chatted playfully with his mother.

Taylor was pleased with his boy's achievements. Jim had built one of the biggest cattle spreads in De-Witt County. But, as he looked on his wife and son, he cursed under his breath. Things had a way of going sour sooner or later and it was happening again.

Earlier that summer the long-running feud with the Sutton family had been rekindled by the killing of Jake Hawkins, a large DeWitt County landowner, rancher, and brother-in-law to Bill Sutton. The fire had raged out of control ever since.

"Get the steak movin', Daddy," Jim said to his father, noting his momentary aloofness and eyeing the pile of chicken-fried tenderloin in front of the rugged Texan.

"What?"

"The meat's gettin' cold, Daddy. Move it on if you ain't gonna have any."

"Oh . . . yeah," the elder Taylor grunted as he stabbed at a piece of the rare, tender beef with his fork and then passed the platter.

The two had argued for two hours before dinner over what course of action they should take. The feud was on the verge of becoming a county war.

"Like I told you before supper. Don't worry none about them Suttons. We'll soon be ending this matter once and for all if my plan works out."

The old man cocked his head back without taking his eyes off his son and then reached around and kneaded his leathery neck. He didn't have his son's enthusiasm for a fight. He knew the price would be too high. The feud had its roots in the War between the States and Pitkin Taylor had been one of the principal hotheads. But the War had been over for more than six years and he was tired of the killing, cattle rustling, and barn burning. Though his hatred for Bill Sutton remained hard and fast in his gut, he saw that the recent renewal of the family vendetta could only lead to disaster. The productivity of their cattle operations was declining, their families were being killed off, their property was being destroyed, and the bankers wouldn't remain understanding forever.

"I'm tellin' you not to worry none, Daddy! Cousin John Wesley and the Clements boys are comin' in this week. I wired them two weeks back."

The table fell silent. It was the first anyone had heard about the arrival of Hardin and the Clements. The elder Taylor fixed his eyes on his son. "I ain't none too pleased to hear that, son."

"Goddamn it, Daddy! This ain't no church picnic we're involved in here. We've put headstones on three of our kin this summer!"

"Jimmy!" his mother snapped. "You'll not be usin' God's name in vain at my table!"

"Don't know, son," Pitkin said calmly, showing no recognition of his wife's reprimand. "Hardin and the

Clements brothers. Almost guaranteed to court trouble. Hell, Wes is wanted, ain't he?"

Jim set his eyes in two thin slits as if squinting into a bright afternoon sun and looked hard at his father. "This here business with them murderin' Suttons has become pretty rough, Pa. Trouble is what *they* been courtin'."

The elder Taylor nodded his head, his sun-baked features showing that he understood his son's position. But his eyes seemed to transmit a sense of sadness, dull and fatalistic.

With a look that would have diverted a tornado, Mary Taylor halted the dinner table talk. When she had their attention, she said gently, "Now there's got to be something better to talk about than this godforsaken feudin'."

Father and son looked at each other, smiled sheepishly, and attacked their dinner. Mary Taylor had a way about her.

The man called Buck hauled his three men up under a stand of live oaks on the northwest side of the well-lit ranch house and proceeded to outline his plan. Once he was sure that they understood, he sent off the dumbest of the trio with a jar of paint and a brush. He had the others circle the house and take up a position in the cornrows on the edge of the large garden. Buck moved in on foot, carefully making his way toward the barn and breeding pens. He heard what he was looking for and made his way toward the sound. After dashing twenty yards, he climbed over the rail fence, unsheathed his knife and cut the leather collar which secured the brass bell to the placid cow.

Pitkin had just carved off a chunk of red meat when he heard the bell and the faint crunching sound.

"Damn," he muttered as he thunked his silverware on the table. "Sounds like one of them cows has got loose again. I'd better fetch her before she tears up the garden."

"I'll tend to it, Daddy," Jim said. "Stay put."

Pitkin put up his hand, palm toward his son. "I'll just be a minute. You and Florence don't get to dinner that often. Sit still and enjoy your Mamma's cookin'." Jim didn't argue. Pitkin Taylor was small but no man to argue with.

When he stepped into the humid night air, he heard the commotion in the cornrows of the family vegetable garden to his left. "Damn," he grunted as he stepped off the porch and paced toward the dull sound of the bell and the noise of the breaking cornstalks.

He hadn't taken ten steps from the porch steps when he saw the flash. A fraction of a second elapsed before he felt the blow. It was as if he'd been kicked in the side by an angry bull. Instinctively he tried to dive for the ground as the air suddenly became permeated with the staccato thumping of rapid-fire gunshots. But he was spinning from a second slug in his shoulder. Then his legs were knocked from beneath him as if he had taken a full-swing blow from an ax handle. The gunfire stopped as quickly as it had started and the damp air was perfectly silent. One leg folded under his body, the old man felt oddly peaceful as he stared at the haze around the moon. Blood seeped from his side, his shoulder, and the gaping rip in his lower leg.

Jim Taylor bolted through the door, nearly unhinging it. His long-barrel Colt .45 drawn, he stopped momentarily and then bounded off the porch in one step and ran to the heap in the earth next to the cornrows. The others streamed out behind him as men began to pour from the bunkhouse.

"God in Heaven!" Jim's mother said as she reached her husband and dropped to her knees. "Why! Why!" she moaned as she looked into his glassy eyes and saw him silently pleading for help.

"What happened?" Jim commanded as he fell to one knee after holstering his Colt.

The old man moved his lips but nothing came out.

"God's sake, son! Get a wagon so we can get him to Cuero."

He jumped up and headed for the barn. It was then that he saw four fast-moving riders cresting the ridge to the northwest. He stopped and shouted at two half-dressed hands who'd run up to him, "There!" He pointed. "Ride those bastards into the earth and bring them back to me." His mother's sobbing caused him to lurch again into a run toward the barn. When he reached the big door he saw the crudely painted sign which sloped downward. The dripping, childlike red letters sent him into a rage.

AN EYE FOR AN EYE. W.S.

"I'll wash my hands in old Bill Sutton's blood!" he snarled as he violently swung the door aside.

TWO

In a rented carriage, Vivian Valentine and Ashley Tallman headed northwest on the Plumb Creek Road. They could have been a banker and his wife out for a morning ride. But they weren't. They were two of Allan Pinkerton's best undercover agents. And they were in Lockhart, Texas, on business.

The morning air was cooler than usual for the last week in August. Violent thunderstorms had moved through during the night, leaving dry, cool air in their wake. Puffy white clouds scooted across the deep blue sky on a stiff breeze. It was almost noon and yet it was only eighty-five in the shade.

Tallman pulled up the single horse when he saw the abandoned settler's cabin two hundred yards to his right. "Looks like the place," he said to Vivian. "Some squatter's dream gone to hell."

Vivian raised her eyebrows at his blatant cynicism but added nothing.

Tallman snapped the reins and turned the dappled gray toward the ramshackle building which seemed to lean toward Plumb Creek as if drawn to the rushing water.

After he'd climbed down and secured reins to a fence post which supported a single broken rail, he helped his partner down. Her scent, her soft hand and long fingers, and his intimate knowledge of what was under her teal blue dress stirred his desire. Vivian was truly one of the most fascinating women he had ever met. As his eye caught the beauty of her flowing auburn hair he sighed and shook his head slowly from side to side.

"What?" she asked, her hazel eyes glistening under the bright sun.

He faked a harsh look and got a chuckle out of her. They both knew *what*. There was an uncommon bond between the two detectives, though it was nothing that resembled the usual man-woman relationship. Truth be known, both were dedicated to personal independence with an intensity that most might have considered a form of madness. But that didn't mean that they would shy from a turn in the hay whenever the occasion arose. Both considered the pleasures of the flesh to be one of Mother Nature's finest inventions. But they understood the boundaries of their personal involvement. And they both had the utmost professional respect for each other.

Tallman had been with Pinkerton since the early days of the Civil War, when he had operated as an undercover agent for the Union Army. Vivian had only joined the agency earlier that spring after Tallman discovered her to be part of a con game he'd been investigating. It was only Tallman's mercy, to hear him tell it, that saved her from a long sentence in the New York State Women's Prison. The truth was, and they both knew it, he was fascinated with her approach to life and her fierce independence, not to mention her beauty, grace, elegance, and voracious appetite for sexual pleasure.

"Pretty spot," she said as she started toward the rain-swollen creek. "I wonder what happened to the settlers who built the little house."

Tallman shrugged.

"Are we early?" she asked as she swept away hair that the stiff breeze had blown in her face.

"A few minutes."

"Do you know much about him?"

"Just that he's the governor of Texas. The first elected since the end of the war."

"I wonder when the Yankees will leave the South to the southerners again?" she asked aloud. Her Virginia heritage made her a partisan of sorts, though she generally wrote off politics as the lowest form of human skulduggery. She had often noted that politics was the art of robbery through deception. "Sherman's troops have been here for more than six years now."

"Probably be here for another six."

"Did Trowbridge go with the South?"

"Don't know," Tallman said as he jammed a thin cigar into the corner of his mouth and went fishing in his vest pocket for a match. "They'll probably stay until the greedy carpetbaggers have sucked the state dry."

Vivian laughed when she saw what Tallman had pulled from his pocket. He fell into a throaty chuckle as he held the one-inch sphere aloft like a magician about to make something disappear.

Their laughter stemmed from a demonstration they'd been given two weeks back by the inventor of the deadly device. Aaron Wagner, Tallman's Chicago gunsmith, had prepared the tiny device with the hope of selling it to the military. It was designed to startle and wound its victim. When tossed against a hard surface, the little ball would erupt in a blast of fire, smoke and metal shards.

"Don't drop that. Remember what happened to Aaron's paper target," Vivian said, pointing toward Tallman's crotch. The target had taken a metal sliver right where the family jewels would normally rest.

Tallman allowed a wry smile, put the dull silver ball away, and pulled out a cheroot.

Vivian watched him fire up his cigar and begin pacing. Her mind soon became cluttered with a desire to strip him naked and ravage his lean, muscular body under the bright sun. No man had ever responded to her unabashed longing for the pleasures of the flesh as had the six-foot-tall, sandy-haired man pacing the creek bank. Though she held the word *love* to be meaningless when employed in its common usage, she had begun to wonder what word might describe her feelings about the man who had crashed in on her bank scam in New York. Whatever it was, it felt good, good for the soul and good for the flesh. She brushed aside the reddish-blond hair the wind had swept in her face and smiled at her own impish designs as she walked toward the cabin.

"This must have been a quaint little home at one time," she said as she stood in the crooked doorway. "But nothing ever stays the same, does it?"

"Nope," Tallman grunted from behind. "One of life's several guarantees."

Vivian walked to the window on the other side of the room and looked out toward the stream.

Tallman caught a whiff of her scent and watched her move across the room. He knew what lay beneath her petticoat and the mere thought of her form sent a surging warmth through his manhood. He groaned to himself as he approached her.

"I love the sound of rushing water," she said as she

turned to face her partner. She reached out and put her hands on his hips.

Tallman smiled, acutely aware of her presence. There was something about the setting that could turn a person's mind toward sex. And he could read Vivian like a book. Her thoughts had taken the same turn.

Her eyes fixed on his, she moved her hands from his waist to the buttons on his trousers. In an instant, her long fingers had found his meaty cock. Her touch made Tallman's member as stiff as a wagon wheel spoke. It always did.

"I don't think the governor expects to meet with us in the nude," Tallman said as Vivian gently fingered the moist tip of his cock.

"Too late now, Ash," she said, almost moaning as she pulled his meat from his fly. "You've got to do something about this," she explained as she bent forward and put the head of his hot member in her mouth. His warmth in her mouth, she felt a tightness in her groin. Ever since her first encounter with a boy, she'd barely been able to satisfy her voracious appetite for sex. Once the feeling began, she had to have her release.

Tallman's knees began to weaken as she sucked at his tip. He reached around, hiked up her skirt and petticoat and worked his hand between her soft thighs. Without hesitation Vivian spread her feet to give Tallman access to her moist cunt. When his fingers found their mark, she shuddered and began pumping his prick at a quickening pace. And when Tallman found her swollen clitoris, he began to circle the hard button with his slick finger.

Moments later, Vivian released his cock, turned toward the windowsill and bent over the opening, all the while careful not to displace Tallman's hold of her cunt. "Ash, I want you inside of me," she moaned as she bent further and pulled her skirt and underthings up over her back. "Deep inside."

Tallman's knees weakened even more when he saw the milky thighs, black garter, dark stockings and red silk underpants. He pulled the red panties aside, exposing the swollen lips of her cunt, which were glistening with her juices. He'd never ceased to be amazed at how wet she got. He stepped forward, and, his right hand holding her pants aside, his left hand holding his cock, he ran the head up and down the length of her juicy slit.

"Ahhhhhhh. Ash. Put it in," she groaned. "Fuck meeeee."

Tallman obliged, slowly pushing his thick cock in to the hilt. Vivian began a slow undulating movement, which quickly began to intensify. Tallman caught the rhythm and began thrusting with her. His desire grew as he looked down and saw his long member, wet with her juices, pumping in and out of her hot cunt. And when Vivian started her animal noises, Tallman grabbed her hips and began to push harder and deeper. Both had now gone over the edge. Pure animal instinct took over their bodies as they approached their release. Vivian felt the first of the pleasurable surges. Then another. Then the hot flood of Tallman's seed filled her cunt. She emitted a high-pitched squeal as they hammered each other to oblivion. Tallman smiled to himself as he became aware that his knees could barely hold him up. He had never been able to figure how his pecker was connected to his knees.

"What's so funny, mister?" Vivian said playfully as she stood up.

"You wouldn't understand," he chuckled.

It was then she heard the carriage. "Oh, damn. The governor's coming."

Tallman stuffed his half-hard meat into his trousers and quickly fingered the buttons in place. "I suppose we both look like we've just run five miles," he said with a grin half a mile wide.

They heard the horse and carriage come to a stop in the front of the cabin.

"Just take a deep breath and smile," Vivian said. "We'll pick up where we left off when we get back to town."

"Governor Trowbridge?" Tallman asked as he stepped through the cabin door.

"Yes, sir!" the large man snapped in a pleasing

tone. Considering his size, he bolted from the buggy with surprising alacrity and extended his meaty hand. "And you must be Mr. Ashley Tallman?"

Tallman nodded and shook Trowbridge's hand firmly yet briefly. Then he turned toward Vivian and added, "Miss Vivian Valentine, my partner."

"My pleasure," Trowbridge said as he tipped his hat and allowed his glance to fall briefly to the twin mounds rising from her light blue dress.

"*My* pleasure, Governor," she said, her voice soft and alluring.

After introductory pleasantries, the governor suggested that they go into the deserted cabin and sit. The trio moved into the building and settled on what remained of the crude furnishings.

"Let's get down to business," the meaty governor said forcefully as he doffed his hat and set it on the marred wooden table. "I've got problems and the sooner I get them straightened out the better I'll rest at night."

After they were all settled, the governor looked toward Vivian, started to say something and then stopped himself.

"Something troubling you?" Tallman asked.

"Well, I . . . to be honest, I must say right off that this Sutton-Taylor business is a rough game, real rough. What I'm tryin' to say is that I have my doubts about a lady gettin' involved."

"I assure you that I can handle myself, Governor," Vivian said, her green eyes fixed on his eyebrows. "This is *my* business and I'm good at it."

"But a lady detective!"

"You might be surprised to learn, Governor, that Allan Pinkerton has a number of lady operatives on the payroll. He has ever since he opened shop." Tallman paused. "They can go places and do things we can't . . . if you get my meaning."

"Well . . . of course," Trowbridge grunted, and looked at Vivian. "Your hide, ma'am!"

"Like you said, Governor, let's get down to business." Tallman stared at the overweight politician and took a long draw on his thin cigar. "We've read your analysis of the feud," Tallman went on, smoke curling from his mouth. "What can you add to that?"

"Hell," Trowbridge growled. "It's gotten a hell of a lot worse since I penned that piece. Five men have died since Pitkin Taylor was dry-gulched. And if he dies, I expect the whole of DeWitt County will go up in smoke."

"That's Jim Taylor's father?" Vivian asked.

"Yes, sir. Of course Bill Sutton swears he had nothing to do with it."

"Who's the local lawman?" Tallman asked.

"Man named Pete Kelly. But he's only one man. You can't lock up the whole goddamn county!"

"What about the Rangers or Sherman's District Five occupation troops?" Vivian asked.

"Politics, Miss Valentine," Trowbridge said bluntly. "Sending Union troops against southerners in Reconstruction Texas would be like playing with matches in a gunpowder factory."

"Why not Rangers undercover?" Tallman asked.

"It's been tried. We lost the man. One of our best too. In fact the day I got the news was the day I called Pinkerton."

"How did he get found out?" Vivian asked.

"Don't know, miss. We just found him tied to a tree with a forty-five-caliber hole in his forehead."

"A Judas?" Tallman asked.

"Can't believe it," Trowbridge shot back. "Only my closest associates knew about it. All trusted men. My guess is it was a fluke."

"I assume that you've sent another man under if you feel that way," Vivian said, her voice cool and calculating. "It's something we've got to know about."

"Frankly, yes. We've got a man inside. Only four people in the world know about it. You make five and six. Of course that's as far as it goes. He's goin' by the name Lem Davis. That's all I know as of now."

"We'll keep a lookout," Tallman said as he thumped out his smoking cigar butt with his boot heel.

Trowbridge went on to explain his problems in some detail. Texas was in a state of relative lawlessness. In some ways the Civil War was still stewing. Bands of unreconstructed Rebs roamed the countryside venting their anger on carpetbaggers, Union sympathizers, freed slaves, lawmen and even on innocent bystanders. The brutal conflict had familiarized the country's young men with the killing lust. Many couldn't stop even though the South had officially surrendered more than six years earlier. Aside from the bitter Rebs, Texas was victim to the crimes of many a hardcase who followed the longhorns. The Sutton-Taylor feudists were icing on the rancid cake.

Early in Reconstruction, in the spring of 1866, Charles Taylor, Pitkin's brother, was set upon by carpetbag officials for whipping a negro after he caught the man snatching a chicken from his pens. Rather than submit to Union law, Charles Taylor became a fugitive and swore to avenge the misdeeds of the carpetbaggers. Within a year he had killed a carpetbagger land speculator, beaten a banker nearly to death with his bare hands, and set fire to the DeWitt County Courthouse during the murder trial of a respected southern army officer who was suspected of leading renegade Rebs in hit-and-run raids against Yankee sympathizers. Though all got out with their lives, the courthouse was reduced to a pile of smoldering ashes within an hour.

A DeWitt County posse led by Bill Sutton had, a month later, captured Charlie Taylor by chance while they were out looking for cattle thieves. In the early A.M. of the second night of his captivity, a group of vigilantes broke Taylor out of jail and hanged him from the ridge pole of the Cuero livery. The identity of Taylor's killers had remained a matter of legend, rumor and speculation. Trowbridge held to the theory that he had been killed by Moshi Tanga and his band of freed slaves. Tanga and his men had roamed the South after the war, seeking retribution for the generations of their families' enslavement. Buck Taylor, a cousin to Pitkin and Charlie, swore that Sutton had something to do with Charlie's lynching. A month after the incident, Buck caught up with Sutton and drew on him. But Sutton beat Taylor and killed him instantly with three well-placed slugs in the chest.

"The way I understood it," Tallman injected, "there was bad blood between the Suttons and the Taylors even before Charlie and Buck were killed. Weren't they accusing each other of cattle thievin'?"

"That's the story," Trowbridge sighed.

"And the feud has had a full head of steam ever since," Vivian added. "I hear the folks back East are even choosing up sides. The magazine writers are having a field day."

Tallman's mind strayed momentarily. Vivian's offhand comment had given him an idea.

"I'm well aware of what the muckrakers are doing with this thing," Trowbridge said, his face reddening. "And more often than not that same type of writer reminds the people of this state that their first elected governor since the war ran his campaign on a law and order theme."

Tallman allowed a thin, dry smile.

"And I'll make no bones about it! The fact is I'm out to save my bacon. That's why I am willing to pay Allan Pinkerton's colossal fees to see if I at least can't get this Sutton-Taylor matter out of my hair."

"The *taxpayers* will get their money's worth, Governor," Vivian suggested with a smile that would cause any man to go weak in the knees.

"You are obviously serious about this matter, Governor," Tallman said, fixing his eyes in a pensive slant. "Just how far do you want us to go?"

"They are all a pack of killers from my point of view. There're no good guys. You do what you have to do. I don't care if you throw away the goddamn lawbooks on this one. I'll back you all the way." Trowbridge paused and pulled at his starched collar and then rubbed his jowls. "Of course it would be better for all concerned if things are kept as quiet as possible."

"Of course," Vivian said, her tone suggesting a complete understanding of the political ramifications of their task.

Tallman nodded approval. "And I assume Pinkerton made it clear that you are the only one who will know about us?" Tallman asked, his angular features commanding assurance. "We work undercover and any leak could buy us six feet of cold dirt." Something in Tallman's face let Trowbridge know that a slip on the governor's part might prove costly.

"That's why we are here in this godforsaken place," Trowbridge grunted, his response ringing with assurance. And it was obvious that the politician didn't appreciate Tallman's implicit warning.

"Just wanted to be sure, Governor," Vivian explained. "It's the secrecy that gives us our edge."

Trowbridge looked at Vivian with a blank stare.

"Do you have any ideas where we might start?" Tallman asked. "A contact. Someone we might approach undercover?" His usual method was to use his mastery of the art of disguise as a way to slip, unnoticed, into the center of the action.

Trowbridge massaged his sagging jowls with his meaty hand as he thought.

"Who would know the most about the feud? Someone in Cuero," Vivian continued. "How about the sheriff? Pete Kelly?"

"Na-a-aw," Trowbridge wheezed. "Kelly's not worth the powder it'd take to blow his nose. But . . . maybe . . . a man named Sheridan Garwood. He's president of the Cuero Safe Deposit Company, the only bank in town. A good man too. Contributor to my campaign. In fact, I believe he has been trying to establish himself as a community peacemaker of sorts. No doubt the feudin' business is bad for banking."

"Sounds interesting," Vivian injected.

"Of course you've got one problem with Garwood."

"What's that?" she asked.

"He's one of those evangelical Christians. I mean one of the real pompous sons of bitches. Always condemning everybody to hell. I believe he's a deacon in the local church."

"Praise the Lord!" Vivian shouted as she threw her arms aloft.

Trowbridge and Tallman exchanged high-eyebrow glances at her antics.

"Aside from this holy man," Tallman asked, "can you think of anyone else? Someone close to the Suttons or the Taylors?"

"Hell, just about everyone in DeWitt County. Fact is, most have taken sides. Those that haven't just want to see the shooting and burning stopped. That is all those except my political enemies. They're having a real horselaugh over the whole thing. The law and order candidate who has no law and order!"

"Any names?" Vivian asked.

"The number one Trowbridge hater is a coyote named Nate Gill. He owns a good piece of the real estate in Cuero. And I think he's raising cows. I guess he's into everything, come to think of it."

"I see," Tallman said, as he went for another cheroot.

"Sorry I can't provide you with any more. I don't personally know any of the Taylors or the Suttons. But I do know you'll have your hands full. It looks like each side is buildin' a damn army. You got John Wesley Hardin, Dick Chisholm, Lefty Walters, Doc Wallis, Johnny Ringo, Sam Bass and Newt Avery just to name a few. The way I see it they would, every one, shoot your grandmother for a silver dollar."

"We know our business, Governor," Vivian chimed in, her self-assurance beaming.

Tallman was amused at her confidence, but her attitude left him somewhat uneasy. The Sutton-Taylor feud was a hornet's nest and getting in and out of a hornet's nest without being stung was damn near impossible.

THREE

As she rode into the outskirts of Cuero on her fancy wagon, she smiled, a big, Christian smile.

"Howdy, sister," a man said from the loading platform in front of the mercantile.

"Gonna save some souls, Miss MacKenzie?" an idler shouted from a crude bench in front of a saloon.

" 'Heaven and earth shall pass away; but His words shall not pass!' " she said to the bench-sitter in a husky tone after holding a hand aloft, her index finger outstretched.

Vivian was suddenly surprised at herself. It had been years since she'd laid a hand on a Bible or set foot in a church or a tent. But she still remembered her Sunday school verses.

It had been a long, hot and dusty ride from Lockhart and she was ready for a hotel room, but she also wanted to make her presence known.

"No better place than here," she muttered under her breath when she saw a drunk stumble out from under a sign—Bank's Saloon and Billiards Parlor—and fall face first into the dusty street.

"Whoa," she said as she pulled up her horse. When the chestnut had settled down, she climbed down and looked around. Cuero was bustling with activity. Teamsters were coming and going with full wagons. The plankwalks were full of farmers, cattlemen, ladies on shopping sprees, and an assortment of idlers. Not to mention the drunk who was now pulling himself up on the water trough under the hitching rail.

It took her only moments to realize that all eyes were quickly focusing on her and on her gawdy wagon. The sturdy oak wagon and the spokes of the wheels had been painted sky blue. The rim and hub of the wheel were a high-gloss black which matched the black trim elsewhere on the rig. White letters outlined in black went the whole length of the wagon's bed, clearly announcing her purpose and profession: THE WAGES OF SIN IS DEATH, ISABELLE MacKEN-ZIE PRAISES THE LORD. She wasn't prepared for the attention and it had momentarily taken her aback. But the temporary confusion caused by the gawking townspeople broke when a young man in a tattered gray suit and a faded black, small-brim Stetson rushed toward her.

"May I help, Miss MacKenzie?" he asked, his approach and demeanor juvenile. "I'm always willing to help when it comes to spreadin' the Gospel."

Vivian wondered about the lad's sincerity when she noticed that his primary concern seemed to be the twin mounds which strained against her plain but neat white blouse. She readily consented though as the crowd thickened. "You may," she agreed. "If you will raise the canvas sides on my wagon I'd appreciate it."

The young man hustled about the gawdy rig, rolled up the three sides and tied them off with the leather thongs hanging from the ornate black trim of the rounded shiplap wooden roof. Before he was finished at least thirty people had gathered. Some stood quietly; others craned their necks; several ladies giggled foolishly. Vivian smiled to herself as she reached inside the wagon for one of the hundred Bibles she had in her fresh inventory. She wished Ash Tallman were there to see the reaction his undercover plan was receiving. Although she had suggested that she might pose as some sort of pompous evangelical in order to approach the banker, Sheridan Garwood, it was Tallman's idea that she ride into town reeking of overstatement. It was in keeping with his theory that the most obvious is the least obvious. When they'd bought the wagon from a busted medicine show operator three days before, she had no idea that her undercover role was going to cast her as the town spectacle.

"All done Miss MacKenzie," the man said, his eyes again straying to her bosom.

"Thank you, ahh . . ."

"Burly Ivans," he responded quickly. "My daddy owns the feed store and we was all a brought up a knowin' Jesus."

"Well! Praise the Lord, Burly. I sure do appreciate your help."

"Anything else I can do, ma'am?"

"You could get down my stand."

Without hesitation the lad reached into the bed of her rig and pulled out her two-foot-by-four-foot stage and placed it at her feet with the speed and deference a servant shows his queen.

Vivian pasted a serious look on her face and mounted the stage, still having no idea what she might say. But she *was* up for the challenge. " 'The wages of sin is death!' " she shouted. The words just came out. Then she saw the drunk who had minutes earlier stumbled out of Bank's Saloon. He was on his knees holding on to the edge of the watering trough with one hand while he splashed water in his face with the other. " 'I am the Alpha and Omega, the beginning and the ending, saith the Lord, which is, and which was, and which is to come, the Almighty!' " Vivian spoke these words from Revelation in a strong and even tone. Though the lines never made sense to her, she'd never forgotten them as her family's preacher had opened every fire and brimstone sermon with those same words.

"You are all going to die!" she shouted as she slapped the new Bible in her palm. "Are you ready? 'For yourselves know perfectly that the day of the Lord so cometh as a thief in the night.'" A strange quiet had come over the semicircular crowd and, for that matter, over the town of Cuero, Texas. She waited and looked, her face in a slight scowl. "Look over there!" She pointed at the kneeling drunk. "Is that man ready to face his maker?" she growled. A passing teamster hauled up his horses to listen. "Or will Satan himself come for that poor soul?" she asked, her voice soft and mellow.

"Hell," someone in the back of the still-growing crowd shouted, "that's old Hawk Joyles. Ain't nobody wants his soul. Not even Satan!"

Raucous laughter overcame the crowd. "You're wrong, sir!" Vivian hollered over the noise. "Satan wants all of you to stoke the eternal fires of hell. On this book I'll promise you that the Devil will carry you off unless you repent of your sinful ways and ask Lord Jesus for forgiveness."

"They got popskull whiskey in heaven, sister?" the same heckler went on. "'Cause if they don't ol' Joyles ain't gonna *want* to go!"

"Shut up Mr. Hayward and let the lady speak God's word," a well-dressed woman said to the heckler.

"Shit, lady," the man sneered. "Everybody knows what's goin' on. She's gonna sell Bibles for ten times what she paid for them and probably pass the god-damn hat to boot!"

Vivian was getting angry at the loudmouth. And that surprised her. She'd so quickly become involved in her little scam that she had almost forgotten that she wasn't a lady preacher.

"Sounds to me, sir, like you ought to be my first customer. Surely seems as if you've got a black heart. The Word will comfort your dark soul." Vivian spoke calmly. Little did she know then how right she was.

"Yeah, Frank," someone shouted across the crowd. "Maybe the Good Book would stop you cheatin' at cards and runnin' up large bills at old Maybell's whorehouse."

This time the crowd's laughter became more bois-terous. They were just settling down when gunshots thumped from within Bank's Saloon. An instant later, two men backed out of the drinking establishment with their revolvers drawn. Then panic set in as one of the gunmen fired his .44 over the batwing doors. The crowd that had been taking in the preacher lady was only fifteen feet from the plankwalk in front of Bank's. Some ran. Others dropped to the dirt. A few watched as if it was a minor curiosity. Vivian stood on her stage, as still as a wooden Indian. She wasn't afraid; she was simply stunned by the suddenness of it all.

Once the two men had mounted their horses, two more backed out, firing their guns through the wooden saloon doors. Under the cover of the two mounted riders, the second pair lurched on to their horses and the four men pounded out of town.

At first the town was dead quiet. Then, slowly, people got up, peeked from behind doors and out of alleyways, and began to chatter quietly as the dust kicked up by the scrambling crowd and the four retreating riders drifted on a breeze, as if to follow the gunmen out of town.

Then a man burst through the bullet-splintered batwings. "Someone get Doc Lee," he bellowed. "We've got three men down in here."

The quiet turned to bedlam as men and women sprinted for the saloon to get a look at the victims. Vivian stepped down and followed, but the small bar and billiards parlor was choked with onlookers before she got there.

In only moments, Doc Lee, a large, gray-haired man, pushed through the blood seekers and shooed the mob aside.

"Who got shot?" a woman asked of one of the men who'd been kicked out by the doctor.

"A couple of drifters—and . . . Bill Sutton," he

answered, his voice accenting Sutton's name clearly.

"My God," the woman shrieked.

"Sutton?" another bystander asked. "Old Bill himself?"

"Sutton himself!" the man confirmed. "Gut shot! Though he ain't dead."

Vivian heard the mood of the crowd change as the name Bill Sutton made the rounds. Some were obviously glad. Others looked somber. But the general tone of the comment seemed to be one of frustration and helplessness. She guessed that the shooting would be a novelty at first but that it would soon sink in that the Sutton-Taylor feud had just taken a nasty turn.

"Back!" the crusty Doc shouted as he led four men who carried a groaning and blood-soaked man in a blanket rigged as a stretcher. "Give these boys some room! Back!"

The rubberneckers fell silent as the glassy-eyed man passed.

"Damned if it ain't Sutton," an old man to Vivian's right muttered after the wounded man had passed. "This here feudin' ain't gonna see no end."

"Did you know Mr. Sutton?" Vivian asked the old-timer.

"Nope, sister. But if you really believe in that prayin' stuff, you'd better say a word or two for him. He don't look too good. And while you're at it, you'd better speak a word or two for this damn town before the war starts." With that, the wrinkled, sun-dried man spat a wad of tobacco juice in the dusty street and left, shaking his head.

"Here comes old Harry!" a man dressed like a storekeeper shouted as if to announce the coming of a circus wagon. "Hell, he's goin' to be a millionaire before this feudin' quits."

Harry Edelbrock, the town's only undertaker and cabinetmaker, pulled up in front of Bank's in his black funeral coach. "Howdy, boys," he said with a plastered grim expression. "Got word that there's business inside."

"That's a fact, Edelbrock," the storekeeper confirmed as Harry climbed from his lofty perch on his hearse. "And you might have to box up Bill Sutton before the sun sets."

"Jeeesus," Harry whistled. "Bill Sutton?"

"Gut shot," the storekeep added.

"Harry, I'd say you had better grab the two inside, get back to your shop, and start makin' boxes," said Frank Hayward, the man who had heckled Vivian earlier. "You are going to have more business than you can handle when the Suttons hear about the old man being gunned down at the poker table by Jim Taylor and his friends."

The undertaker grew wide-eyed, nodded slowly, and then walked through the bullet-splintered doors.

Vivian was surprised at the heckler's obvious amusement over the spilled blood. He seemed to have an odd sense of satisfaction on his face and in his voice. As she worked her way around to the well-dressed man who'd been accused of running up large bills at Maybell's, she decided that he was most likely being human. When she moved in next to the heckler, he turned and seemed surprised.

"Well, if it ain't the preacher lady!"

She eyed him with a moderate scowl and was about to say something nasty when a commotion at the saloon door caused all heads to turn. Four men were hauling a body out through batwings under the supervision of Harry Edelbrock. The corpse had the smell of death and looked worse. The young victim had taken a slug in the left side of his face. A gaping hole in the right side of his head was a mass of gray pulp and bone splinters matted to sticky hair.

"Well, now," the heckler, Frank Hayward, said again as he turned toward Vivian, "looked like that boy could have used one of them Bibles of yours."

"You seem to be taking all this in stride, sir," she said in a curt voice. Her disgust showed through. "And it seems to me that you've always got something to say about everything, Mr.—"

"Hayward, ma'am. Frank Hayward. And I was enjoying your fine sermon there until our little shoot-out mucked up everything."

"I took notice of your enjoyment, Mr. Hayward, and I am not sure I appreciate that kind of fun."

"Don't hurt none for a body to have a little fun now and again. Even that mean old god of yours wouldn't take that away from us . . . or would he?"

"My God is a compassionate god, sir!"

"I don't know, ma'am. Looked to me like you was about to send Hawk Joyles straight to hell just before the shootin' started," Hayward said, his voice smooth and overflowing with confidence. "And you can be sure I won't come down too hard on the Lord, Miss MacKenzie. Just on the outside chance there's something to it." Hayward rested his hand on an unusually well-oiled, long-barrel revolver and smiled.

Vivian was intrigued by the cleanly dressed, neatly manicured man. She sensed that he was something more than the town blowhard. She considered herself a master con artist and, in fact, she'd proved that many times before she'd run into Tallman on her last con. She decided to press him for more. "I noticed that you said Jim Taylor was one of the men who shot these fellows?" she asked in a softer tone as she allowed her alluring eyes to settle on his. "Don't tell me this has something to do with that awful family feud that's been in all the papers?"

"Same one, miss."

"How awful."

"And it's hardly a feud anymore. War might be a

better word," he said, his voice radiating a sense of satisfaction.

"A war! What on earth makes you say such a thing?" she exclaimed, sounding like an innocent young girl.

The four body handlers went back into the saloon. Edelbrock followed, his pasted somber expression still intact.

"Hell, Miss MacKenzie, a bunch of people have died in the last couple of weeks. It's more 'an feudin', especially when you consider the troops that are fighting now."

"I'm not sure I understand, Mr. Hayward."

"You don't know who the other three were with Jim Taylor?"

"No, I'm afraid I don't."

Hayward smiled as he lifted his clean Montana-peak Stetson and reseated it. "The one in the buck-skin vest was Taylor's cousin, John Wesley Hardin, and the other two was the Clements boys."

"Never heard of them," she lied.

"Where you been, sister?" Hayward asked, obviously surprised. "They are three of the meanest gun-slicks ever to ride these parts."

"Outrageous! And they just walk into town and shoot people? Where's the sheriff?"

"Pete Kelly ain't no match for those boys. Besides, this is Texas and the law can only do so much. Kelly knows he'd soon be in one of Edelbrock's four-dollar boxes if he interfered."

Just as the undertaker's helpers came off the plankwalk with another body, Vivian caught sight of a lone rider loping toward the edge of the crowd on a dusty, tired-looking paint. She thought she saw a thin smile under the rider's beard stubble and the heavy layer of trail dust, which looked like it had been baked on.

Tallman *was* smiling, though he was trying hard not to show it.

FOUR

When Vivian heard the knock on the door and then the familiar voice, she let Tallman in. Though the sun would be up in four hours, they were both very much awake.

"Damn, cowboy," she said, squinting her eyes and holding her nose. "Don't you ever take a bath?"

Tallman grunted and tossed his hat on the scratched and gouged chair at the foot of the brass bed. A small cloud of dust erupted when the sweat-stained hat hit the wooden seat.

He'd hung around Bank's all afternoon and most of the night trying to reconstruct the shooting. But the circuslike atmosphere and the drunken eyewitnesses made the gusty tales nearly incomprehensible. And to add to his souring mood, he was going to sleep in the loft of the livery in order to maintain his cover as Turk Willis, a penniless, blackhearted Reb drifter who'd shoot a man for a ten-dollar gold piece. He was in no mood for jokes about his odor.

"Well now, preacher lady," he said as he dropped his six-foot frame in the upholstered chair next to the door. "Turk Willis sure as hell wouldn't smell like a goddamn petunia, would he?" It was then that he noticed that Vivian *did* smell like spring flowers.

"Drink?" she asked.

"Two or three," he grunted.

Vivian got a bottle out of her carpetbag and poured two hefty portions of Tallman's favorite Kentucky sour mash. She handed one to him and hoisted hers aloft. "To the Suttons and the Taylors," she said. "May they rest in peace, someday soon."

Tallman nodded his approval and slugged the expensive whiskey. Vivian sipped hers and then took his glass to the washstand to refill it. He felt a tension in his loins as he watched her hips move under her white silk robe. He still had a clear recollection of her firm upsloping breasts, her long and trim legs, and the soft auburn triangle that covered the gate to her womanhood. And he'd never met a woman who got as wet as she did. And that was saying something.

Under the layer of dirt, dried sweat, and stubble was a man who could inflame any woman's desire. Ash Tallman had an animal magnetism which drew women his way and caused them to beg for his attention. And he rarely refused a woman's advance. He enjoyed life's finer pleasures and saw no reason why a man should not reap the harvest before the worms feasted on his own flesh. He was approaching forty and the years were passing at a quickening pace.

"What did you find out?" Vivian asked, backing away and then sitting on the goose-down bed. "Did you figure out how to solve a family feud?"

"That little thought passed by your mind too?" he asked, glad to hear that she shared his bewilderment. "It's one thing to bring down crooks, holdup artists, bunco operators and rotten politicians. But it's something else, the more I think on it, to solve a family feud which has gone haywire."

"I know. The thought hit me today as I watched that odd-looking undertaker pull away from Bank's with his bodies."

"It may come down to simply putting the principals out of action."

"Do you mean what I think you mean?" she asked.

Tallman smiled, shrugged and took a quick pull on his whiskey. "You heard Trowbridge. He wants it stopped."

Vivian paused and looked into the amber fluid in her glass. She dropped the subject and asked Tallman what he'd found out at Bank's.

"Not much. By the time I got settled in, the story had been embellished to the point where it was barely coherent. Best I could figure was that Taylor, Wes

Hardin and the Clements brothers went into Bank's to shoot Bill Sutton. The two dead men were a couple of Sutton's hired hands. Hired gunmen, not cattle drovers."

"I gather they weren't too adept at their trades considering that they've been suited up in pine."

"There aren't many who can hold their own against Hardin and the Clements."

"Not if their reputations have any validity," Vivian added. Then she thought of the odd reactions of the townspeople. She grew pensive as if she'd lost her train of thought.

"What?" Tallman asked when he saw her distant look.

"Nothing really. I was just recalling some of the strange reactions I observed when the locals were hovering over the blood and guts. Some acted the way you might expect. But others seemed to enjoy the whole thing like a little kid would enjoy a carnival. It gave me the willies."

"You too," Tallman sighed as he took another pull on his whiskey. "I did manage to find out that some of the ranchers are getting behind on their accounts. Some pisswillie kid who claims his daddy owns the grain store was pretty loose-mouthed about his father's business. Of course I oiled him up with several glasses of brew."

"Burly Ivans?"

"That was his name."

"Yes. I met him today. Seemed like a nice young lad," Vivian said with a sultry look. "And there you go, leadin' him to the ways of the devil."

Tallman sipped his whiskey, raised his eyebrows, and allowed a startled expression. "Nice lad for sure! When he wasn't blowing off about his old man's business affairs, he was rambling on about how he'd like to have a taste of what was between the legs of the new preacher lady in town."

"Hmm," Vivian groaned with an inviting smile. "I guess my little helper was not as much of a Christian as he claimed. Of course, he was being corrupted by the devil's drink."

"Oh, he might be a Christian, but that doesn't mean he couldn't get weak-kneed over a tender beauty like Isabelle MacKenzie."

Vivian struck a dramatic pose on the edge of the bed. " 'And when the woman saw that the tree was good for food, and that it was pleasant to the eyes, and a tree to be desired to make one wise, she took of the fruit thereof, and did eat, and gave also unto her husband; and he did also eat. And the eyes of them both were opened, and they knew that they were naked.' " Then she drained the last of the whiskey from her glass and fixed her eyes on Tallman. She seemed to have a serious expression, an intense but momentary look of concern. It was a look he had seen only rarely. Then it vanished. She popped off the bed and went quickly to the washstand for a refill.

"How the hell do you remember all those Bible verses anyhow?" Tallman asked.

"I've told you about my strict upbringing in the Virginia aristocracy," she said, her intense expression having given way to the normal, relaxed air which marked her character. "Bible reading was an everyday chore. After dinner, my father would quiz us on our verses. Swift and severe punishment would follow *any* failures. It was much simpler to memorize the words. Oddly enough, they're still there."

Tallman had heard the basic story. Yet he was always amused when it was embellished with another detail. He found her lack of guilt to be the most fascinating part of her character. After running away from home at seventeen, she'd led a purple life as a con artist. She'd openly sought the pleasures of the flesh, good food, good drink and ravenous sexual encounters with men who appreciated the same.

"Those quiz sessions were usually held just before Daddy made his evening rounds of the slave quarters," she added. "Just before he had one of his exotic little slave girls."

Tallman smiled gently. "Day by day and sooner or later six feet of dirt."

"I've heard it before." She chuckled, her face suddenly bright again. Even though he looked as if he'd been dragged from Lockhart behind a horse, she knew what lay beneath the disguise. She wanted him and it showed.

"What did you find out about Garwood?" he asked, after another slug of whiskey. "Did you get to meet him?"

"First thing tomorrow," she answered. "I'm going to ask to do a guest sermon at the Cuero Baptist Church."

"*I* might even go to church to hear *that*."

Vivian disregarded his remark and went on to explain what she'd uncovered. After the shooting, she had checked into the town's only hotel, the Gulf. The three-story building was nothing special, but the worn furniture and bed linens were clean. And it had a bath in each of the rooms on the first and second floors. When she had expressed her surprise, the desk clerk had explained that Mr. Nathan Gill owned the hotel and that he'd had a plumber from Austin outfit the rooms with tubs which were fed by a thousand gallon cask on the third floor. The water, the man had explained, was pumped up by a steam engine. When she'd heard the name Gill, she'd listened carefully to the man's story about plumbing and then got him talking about his boss. It hadn't taken her long, using her womanly charm, to extract a wealth of information about the governor's number one DeWitt County enemy.

Gill had become one of the county's principal land speculators right after the war. Having arrived from Scotland in 1865, he'd managed to avoid having any allegiance to the North or the South. Though he didn't currently have any cattle interests, contrary to the governor's claims he'd recently started to purchase rangeland to add to his DeWitt County holdings.

"Has he taken sides in the feud?" Tallman interrupted.

Vivian explained that he hadn't and that she'd assumed that it made good business sense since he owned Bank's Saloon, the Gulf Hotel, one of the farm supply stores and several other buildings which he leased to other businesses, including Maybell's Dance Hall, the town's only whorehouse. With everyone taking sides he'd only lose, if he declared for one family or the other.

"Sounds right," Tallman added after lighting up a cigar.

She saw that his glass was empty and she quickly took it to the washstand for a refill. "This whole Sutton-Taylor feud could be the best thing in the world for someone like Gill," she said, handing the glass back to Tallman, her white silk robe opening further to reveal her sheer silk nightgown. "Sooner or later these families are going to kill each other off, and . . ."

"Someone like Gill will be around to pick up the pieces at five cents on the dollar. Not to mention that the whole thing happens to be a burr under the governor's saddle and Gill is the primary advocate of the other party in DeWitt County." Tallman chuckled as he usually did when he mused on the misfortunes of one politician or another. "Looks like this Gill fellow is running some lucky cards."

"I'd say so," she said as she again settled on the edge of the bed.

"Did you find anything on Garwood?"

"Not much more than the governor told us," Vivian answered. "Cuero Safe Deposit is the only bank in town and he is the majority stockholder. But he's best known for his constant effort to bring the citizens of Cuero to his brand of Christianity. My cover should be perfect."

"What about his involvement in the feud?"

"Peacemaker. Just like Trowbridge said. Guess he is forever trying to quell the fighting. I gather he has set up several meetings and even claims to have kept the peace for three months before Pitkin Taylor was gunned down in his front yard."

Fatigue and the whiskey were taking their toll on Tallman. He'd been only half listening. And an intimate knowledge of what lay under the pale blue silk nightgown was the ultimate distraction.

"I guess that was what broke it wide open again," she added. "What will be—"

Tallman got up and walked to the door, interrupting Vivian. "You pursue Garwood and I'll see if I can hire out to one of the two families." He was blunt and his voice was a monotone. "In the event of trouble or a change of plans, I'll return to the Longwood Hotel in Lockhart and register as Leroy Bentham. We'll code the case *Isaiah's Glory.*"

"What fired you up all of a sudden?" she said as she got up and retrieved her partner's dirty hat. As she approached, her white robe fell open revealing two firm and large breasts under pale blue silk. "You don't have to run off. You sure you don't want to sample the only piped-in bathtub in southeastern Texas? Just like Chicago."

Tallman was tempted. "Better get your beauty sleep and bone up on your Bible verses so you will dazzle Garwood tomorrow . . . or today. Whatever." It was four A.M. He snitched a glance at her breasts and caught her naughty-girl look when he looked up. He remembered the firmness of her tits. "Like I said," he went on, "who'd believe my cover if I scrubbed up and smelled of lilac water?"

"Even bums on the owlhoot soak in the stream or the livery's horse trough every now and then," Vivian said as she walked up to him, her chest thrust forward. "Now, sit down and relax while I pull off your boots."

Tallman allowed a broad smile, sat down and thrust a foot forward. Suddenly, he didn't need any convincing. The sight of her moist lips, a whiff of her scent, and the prospect of a bath collapsed his will.

"Jesus! Hot water!" Tallman exclaimed as he lowered himself into the big, round oak strake tub. "A hot bath in Cuero, Texas."

"The funny little clerk told me they have copper coils in the chimney of the hotel cook stove," Vivian said as she slipped out of her silk nightgown. Then she fetched soap and a washrag and climbed into the tub with Tallman. "Crowded, I'd say."

"We'll make do," Tallman said, his desire for sleep having given way to the warm throbbing in his cock.

Vivian began soaping her breasts, slowly kneading the firm flesh as her nipples grew erect. Tallman took it all in with his usual delight. He never failed to be amazed at her ability to inflame a man's desire. He'd been around and sampled the pleasures of many women. Most could easily light the fire for a time or two. But it took a special woman to keep an experienced man interested, a woman who knew how to dig down in a man's soul and find the animal and then release the beast.

Tallman brought his knees up and lay back against the wall of the tub. Vivian's hand cupped his balls gently with one hand as she began to stroke his submerged cock with the other. Tallman closed his eyes as he felt himself rising quickly to his release. He knew what Vivian would do. She wanted to get him off in the tub and then take him to the goose down, where she'd suck him until she had it as stiff as an ax handle. Then she'd ride his shaft to a succession of jolting releases. The anticipation pumped a shot of adrenaline into his blood and started his heart pounding.

Vivian felt her cunt throbbing as she pumped Tallman's stiff meat. She unabashedly released her hold on his balls and slid two fingers into her cleft when she felt Tallman nearing his release. She decided that the sun would be up before she'd had enough.

FIVE

It was nine o'clock before Vivian stirred. She woke up suddenly, surprised by the sounds in the street. Two floors below, the town was teeming with activity and a gentle, warm breeze filled the sun-faded flowery curtains. The *clip-clop* of walking horses, the rattle of freight wagons, and the chatter of people created a symphony which commanded her to arise and attack the day.

She slowly swung her feet to the threadbare carpet and wiped her eyes. A quick look about the room made her ask herself why she submitted to such primitive conditions when there were places like Chicago, San Francisco, Boston and New York. But whenever she asked herself that question, the answer was always the same. She loved the con, not to mention the danger. And working for Pinkerton allowed her to play her games on the right side of the law.

The sight of the small tubroom door eased the pain.

After a long bath and a late breakfast, Vivian left the Gulf and stood momentarily on the plankwalk under the warm sun. Cuero didn't look like a town with trouble. She then adjusted her dark blue bonnet and headed south on DeWitt Street, the town's main thoroughfare. The Cuero Safe Deposit Company was three doors away. Like most buildings in Cuero, the bank was a wooden frame building. The façade was carefully manicured, darkly stained vertical board-and-batten and rust-red trim. Gold leaf letters on a heavy glass window spelled out the bank's name. The neat building was directly across from Nate Gill's real estate office.

Vivian took a deep breath and entered. "Is Mr. Garwood in?" she asked the teller in a crisp and commanding voice.

"Yes, ma'am," the slender, bespectacled teller said as he nodded in the direction of an open-top cubicle enclosed in frosted glass.

She walked toward the office with purpose in her steps. At the door, she rapped sharply with her knuckles.

"Come in," a husky voice responded.

Vivian stepped inside with a determined look on her face.

"May I help you?" Garwood asked as he popped

out of his chair and extended his hand once he saw that it was the preacher lady who'd caused the stir the day before.

"I'm Isabelle MacKenzie," she lied. "I'd like to talk with you about a matter of great importance to all of us."

"Of course, Miss MacKenzie. I managed to stick my head out the door of the bank yesterday just after you started your fine sermon. Sorry you didn't get further before the Lord's work was so rudely interrupted by the devil's doin'."

"May God triumph," Vivian added.

With that, both launched into a frenzy of small talk about the winning of souls. Though Garwood appeared to be a gasbag when it came to his Christian pronouncements, Vivian sensed that there was more to the man than met the eye. Unlike most Bible thumpers she'd ever known, Garwood appeared self-assured and very secure in the ways of the secular world. In fact she thought he looked more like a high-class riverboat gambler than a bank president. Though he was probably over forty, he sported a head of thick curly brown hair and his face looked younger; his eyes seemed to reveal that he had an uncommon lust for life and its finer things. His bushy eyebrows moved as if to accent his animated talk. And his sun-darkened skin appeared pliable and soft. Vivian saw something she liked and began to wonder if vamping Garwood might be more pleasure than work. In any event, she was pleased that he wasn't a slob.

"It looks as if you have your work cut out for you in Cuero," Vivian said, continuing their conversation, angling toward the feud. "If my eyes don't deceive me, it appears that Satan has decided to camp right here until he destroys your town."

"Yes, we do have a problem," Garwood agreed. Though his voice didn't seem to mirror any great concern. "Half of the county must be bogged down in this Sutton-Taylor mess. I've tried to act as a go-between, a peacemaker of sorts. But without much success, I might add."

"What's it all about?" she asked, settling back and crossing her legs. Her dark blue skirt, billowing slightly with a small petticoat, shifted and allowed Garwood a peek at her black-stockinged calves. "How did it all get started?"

Garwood's primitive instincts stirred when he saw Vivian's lower leg. Though she was dressed in a plain, highly starched, white blouse, Garwood had visions of what she would look like in the nude, stretched out on a blanket next to a quiet stream under the rays of the noon sun.

Had she been capable of reading his mind at that moment, she would have understood why his tan appeared so even. He loved to get naked under the hot Texas sun.

Garwood pushed aside his lustful thoughts and began to explain the feud, hoping to impress the glowing beauty with his knowledge of the Sutton-Taylor affair. He'd already decided that he wanted to see more of Isabelle MacKenzie.

Vivian thought it odd that he almost seemed to take pleasure in the tale. He was more like someone telling ghost stories to little kids than a banker recounting a tale of woe which was on the verge of destroying a town, a county, and possibly influencing the next gubernatorial election. She wrote it off to his vanity and pressed further.

"What about the law?" she asked. "Do people just ride into town and kill people? And then ride out? No one even took a shot at those killers yesterday."

"Mostly, folks are scared," Garwood explained. "Many people have taken sides. Some are fed up and want nothing to do with it. *They* don't care if the families kill each other off. As for the law . . . that's Pete Kelly. He's one man who isn't about to take up arms against half of DeWitt County. And, of course, no one blames him."

"But it must be hurting business in town," she said.

"No doubt about that. I can attest to it," Garwood replied, impressed that Isabelle had some small feel for commerce. "Remember, I'm the banker. Farmers at war don't plant and harvest crops. Likewise, ranchers don't move cows. No revenues ... no interest payments. The bank is beginning to feel it. You might say my interest in the feud goes beyond the bounds of Christian charity."

"I see," Vivian said, hesitant about giving approval of his commercial concerns.

"You know," Garwood said, "I don't know why you came to see me." He was hoping to get her back on a Christian track so that he might ask her out for the evening. "I feel as if I have been rude."

"Oh, you haven't," Vivian said honestly. "I've found the story captivating. Of course you realize that the Sutton-Taylor business has made the papers back in St. Louis? And further east I've heard."

"I am aware of that," he said as he fingered his bow tie. "You are from St. Louis?"

"Virginia originally. But our mission is headquartered in St. Louis. The Herald Bible Mission."

"There will never be enough Bibles as long as Beelzebub is on the loose!"

"Praise the Lord! The Word is what the mission is all about. And that is why I came to you. You are one of two contacts I was given. We approach outstanding Christian citizens of the communities we serve and ask for help from the local churches. Reverend Thomas Tripp of the Cuero Methodist was the other."

She'd gotten Tripp's name from the four-page morning paper.

"Well! That's flattering. I may be able to help you at Cuero Baptist, but you'll have to see Tripp about the Methodists. Needless to say we don't get on very well with the Methodists."

"Oh?"

"All the trappings, higher-ups, the national organization . . ."

"That is a problem we have. Of course the mission is nondenominational. And I must say that the Lord must look on us with disfavor when he sees our squabbling. After all, we all read the same Bible."

"I'll be glad to see what I can do for you. Just name it."

"Thank you, Mr. Garwood. Though I am sure your Baptists all have Bibles, I'd like to preach a sermon to all the congregations in Cuero before I move on. I might be able to place a copy of the Good Book with a new family member or someone who's just moved to town. And of course I would like to say a few words about how the unity of Christians might be achieved by a closer adherence to the Word."

"And to pass the plate?" Garwood asked.

"Of course," Vivian said bluntly when she saw a knowing glimmer in his brown eyes. "The coin in the platter is what we live on. And we do leave Bibles in hotel rooms, mining camps, logging camps, and with railroad construction crews. It all calls for a modicum of charity."

"I understand," he said, trying not to reveal that he thought Isabelle MacKenzie's Bible operation was a total con. Garwood knew everyone had an angle. He did. And he smiled inwardly as he pulled his watch from the dark gray vest which matched his jacket and trousers. "I'm sorry, Miss MacKenzie, but I must get to a meeting," he noted truthfully. "I want to talk to you further. Would you accept an invitation to dinner? The steakhouse next door has the finest beef in Texas."

She readily accepted.

"Seven?"

"Fine. I'm in room two-oh-three at the Gulf."

SIX

Tallman stood at the wooden bar and looked over
the crowd. Several tables were full of pensive
card players. One billiard table was the center of a
loud game. While two slicks poked at the multicol-
ored balls with their cue sticks, onlookers hooted and
howled through whiskey breath and took up side bets
on each shot. A three-piece band hammered out a
tune which he did not recognize. Though their style
was odd, it was catchy. As he sipped his draught, he
wondered how the three black musicians got along in
Reconstruction Texas. In any event, they seemed to
enjoy their music. The piano player stroked the keys
with deft fingers. The man on the upright bass
seemed to be in a state of ecstasy as he pulled at the
large strings while the huge man seated behind a single snare drum and a high-hat cymbal moved his lips

and looked off into infinity as his sticks tapped a perfect backbeat. Tallman was enjoying the evening in spite of his grubby clothes and itchy stubble.

"Another ale, mister?" the barkeep asked after Tallman thunked his empty glass on wood.

"Yep," Tallman grunted as he mused that everything in Bank's bar looked worn, marred or broken. He didn't feel out of place. It was obvious that Cuero couldn't support a high-class joint even if it could be in character. Of course, it wouldn't.

The barkeeper slid the mug toward Tallman, slopping ale over the rim of the glass. "Five cents," he said, his eyes cast aside as if he was looking at a spot on the bar.

Tallman slapped a half-dollar on wood and turned back toward the musicians.

"Where are you from?" a carefully dressed man asked.

"No place special," Tallman replied, noting that the intruder was dressed like a cleaned-up, pressed and combed version of a cattle drover, a dry goods store dummy dressed in western wear.

"Ooo. One of them," the stranger groaned. "No need to get testy, partner. I was just trying to make talk." Then the man laughed aloud, as if he'd just recalled a joke told a week before.

"Somethin' strike you funny, mister?" Tallman

asked, putting on his best Georgia accent and boring into the slicker's eyes with his hateful stare.

"Whole goddamned world strikes me funny, partner. 'Specially these times . . . what with the Yankees still running Texas after the war's been over for better than six years." The man had picked up on Tallman's accent and was trying to befriend him.

But Tallman remained silent and sipped his ale. Something bothered him about his newfound drinking partner. He was more than a little out of place. His slightly faded red and black check shirt was so neat that one would have expected that his lady'd spent two hours ironing it. His leather vest was obviously as expensive as his custom boots and the gun leather which held a clean and well-oiled .44-caliber Smith & Wesson Model 1869 American. Then Tallman noticed that the man's Levi's were even ironed. He decided to humor the stranger. "Who'd you fight with?" Tallman asked.

"Pickett's artillery at Manassas. And I stayed with them until the end. That is, until *my* end. When it was obvious it was all over, I got the hell out and made for Mexico before the bluebellies could lock me up in one of them stinkhole prisons." The stranger sipped his beer. "How about you?"

"Georgia regulars. Infantry." Tallman lied. But he knew what he was talking about. As a Pinkerton in the hire of the Union Army, he'd infiltrated Colonel Fisher's Georgia regulars and provided the Union with valuable information on fighting strength and troop movements.

"You got a name?"

"Turk Willis."

"Frank Hayward," the other man said. "Drink up and have the next one on me."

Tallman nodded thanks and drained his glass.

After several mugs of beer, Tallman got Hayward talking about the Bill Sutton shoot-out. The tall, well-dressed stranger spoke lovingly of the whole affair. He told the Sutton-Taylor story as if he was equally proud of both sides and he seemed to have a historian's eye for detail. Tallman was gleaning information that he'd not heard before. But he surmised, after listening to the talk and recalling the jabber of the day before, that the feud had made Cuero a national landmark, that most were just proud to have their jerkwater town in the national eye. And the *Cuero Democrat* had devoted the whole front page of that morning's paper to the Bank's shoot-out.

As they talked, Tallman, an actor who'd hold his own in any stage production, pried more information from the slickly dressed Frank Hayward. Allowing himself to appear to be a slow-witted drifter who delighted in Hayward's tall tales and ready access to the details of the feud, he slowly got the inside track on Hayward.

As the evening grew older, the three black men became more radical in their music. They'd start with some basic tune and slowly move into odd-sounding progressions of that basic theme. Though by midnight no one cared. In fact the music fit the other noises that echoed in the bowels of Bank's Saloon and Billiards Parlor, especially the noises made by one group of championship drinkers at a corner table. The quartet of hardcases was drinking popskull whiskey like a cowpuncher would slug water under the summer sun. Two saloon girls, though seeming to take it as another day's work, were getting the worst of it. One of the four men, the apparent ringleader and chief blowhard, was mauling the prettier of the two girls to a degree which bordered on assault. The man's manners had begun to distract Tallman from Hayward's windy accounts of the feudists' earlier battles. The young girl's face had been transformed to a mask of fear in the previous half hour. Twice the meaty ringleader had pulled one of the girl's breasts from her skimpy dress and pressed her brown nipple into his bearded face. From the sound of her shrieks he was biting her, and the second time she'd pulled away, he'd held her slender neck in a stranglehold until her face got white.

"Who's the fat scum tryin' to choke the little girl," Tallman asked Hayward when the thug had put another chokehold on the girl.

"Tinker Morton. And you'll notice there ain't no one who's about to stop him."

Tallman had noticed that, although many were looking toward the loud table with disgust in their expressions, no one seemed anxious to intervene. He saw an opportunity in the girl's misfortune.

"I see that," Tallman said in a level tone. "What makes his fat ass so special?"

"Damn near three hundred pounds and that ivory-handle pigsticker on his belt. Some say he's fast enough to cut out a man's heart and feed him a piece before he dies."

The ham-fisted hulk released the girl when her face got white and again forced her large, youthful breast into the folds of his black beard while his trio of followers laughed as the girl screamed.

"What's he do when he ain't cuttin' out hearts?" Tallman asked Hayward in a mocking tone. "Keep charge of the church charities?"

Hayward and two others at the bar chuckled at Tallman's remark.

"Mostly he just hangs around and makes trouble for the Taylors or their kin. He was boasting three days ago that he wants to be the man that kills John Wesley Hardin and the Clements boys."

"They're the cousins of Jim Taylor that rode with him yesterday?"

"The same," Hayward answered.

"That makes the woman beater partial to the Suttons?"

"Might say that. Though I doubt Bill Sutton would admit to Tinker Morton bein' on his side . . . if you get my drift. Sutton's got limits. If he's still alive."

Tallman sipped his beer and noticed that the room was getting quieter by the minute as the fat man further abused the girl while one of the others pawed the other saloon girl.

"I told you that most have chosen sides," Hayward added.

Tallman's utter disgust over Morton's antics was growing intense. And, in the past, he'd found that there was no better way to get an invite into criminal circles than to flatten the face of a blowhard like Tinker Morton.

"I can see what you're thinkin', Turk," Hayward said bluntly. "If you want Morton, you'd better back-shoot him with a sixty-two caliber buffalo gun . . . while he's sleepin'."

Tallman looked at Hayward and smiled, a dumb but evil grin. "Come to think of it, Frank, I ain't heard you declare sides in the feud," Tallman asked, changing the subject, hoping to learn whether or not he and Morton might be on the same side.

"You ain't, and you ain't likely to. I'm happy to watch and pick up some of the pieces after it is all over!"

Hayward's self-assured and matter-of-fact claim that he would be on the cleanup committee took Tallman by surprise. It was an angle he wouldn't have attributed to Hayward.

"Makes sense. Can't say as I—"

"Aaahh!" the saloon girl screamed.

Tallman spun away from the bar to see Morton tear the bargirl's dress off. The young woman stood clothed only in her garter and panties and black net stockings, shuddering with terror, sobbing with resignation. Tinker Morton picked her up and stood her on the table. The saloon had become dead quiet save the verbal antics of Morton and his drunken trio of toughnuts.

"Whatch gonna do, Tink," one of the drunks asked, his smile revealing a gum full of what looked more like cloves than like teeth.

"Now little lady!" Morton shouted. "Why don't you give the boys a little thrill and dance." Then he turned to the silent musicians. "You three cotton pickers! Strike me up a goddamn tune! Now!"

Before Morton had turned back, the band began to stroke out a halfhearted tune which sounded like a cross between a minuet and a march.

Tallman set his beer on the scarred bartop and started forward.

"Don't mix in, Turk," Hayward said as he grabbed Tallman's arm. "You got ten glasses of beer talkin' to you. Must be! 'Cause it couldn't be your good sense."

Tallman stopped and turned toward Hayward. "I assume that newfangled Smith hogleg you're carryin' is more than decoration. Just keep them three off me while I give that dog shit Morton a lesson in manners."

Tallman was hoping he had read the situation right. Morton was obviously drunk. And he read Hayward as a capable man with a revolver. If he could mop the floor with Morton, he guessed he might get an invite into one of the warring camps. He had little else to go on and, regardless of the outcome, he loved an occasional skullbuster, especially with an ape like Morton.

"Here you skinny slut," Morton growled as he handed the white-faced girl an empty whiskey bottle. "While your dancin' put this somewhere so's you'll give the boys a thrill . . . and maybe yourself too!" Morton exhaled a huge laugh. After a moment the three sidekicks joined in. Other than the halfhearted noise from the band, the room was quiet. Some men watched, others went on with their business. A few left.

Tallman strode quickly to confront the smelly Morton, snatching an empty bottle from a table. "How about you stick this whiskey bottle up your ass, fatman," Tallman growled as he held the bottle toward Morton. "Maybe give your own self a thrill. You look like the kind of ignorant bastard that would enjoy something stiff up your shitter!"

The band stopped.

Several patrons snickered.

The room got as quiet as a funeral service.

Morton's eyes were instantly frozen with rage.

Tallman took a step forward and thrust the bottle out. "Well, lard-ass, drop your britches. Or do I have to drop them for you?"

With that, Morton charged like an enraged bull. At the last instant, Tallman stepped aside and tripped him. Morton hit the floor face first, going down like a stunned cow in a slaughterhouse. Slowly, Morton got to his knees and then to his feet. He had the smile of a kid who'd just been given free run of the mercantile candy counter.

"Well, fatman," Tallman said, coldly waving the bottle toward Morton.

Again Morton charged. He appeared suddenly sober and determined. With careful aim Tallman threw the bottle right at the bull's face. It hit on the man's right eyebrow, opening a two-inch gash, causing blood to flow over Morton's face. But the blow from the bottle didn't even slow Morton down. Tall-man met him with three left jabs to his cut eyebrow. But they were not enough to stop Morton's round-house right. Though the blow was wild, it caught Tall-man in the left arm and sent him reeling into a poker game. The cheap round table broke and Tallman went to the floor in an explosion of cards, coin, and bank-notes. His arm felt paralyzed. Before he had his senses, Morton approached slowly with the deadly smile still pasted between his overgrown black mus-tache and beard. Tallman started to roll away, but Morton's giant boot had stomped him in the chest be-fore he knew what happened. Then he saw the foot coming toward his face. His survival instinct overrul-ing his stunned arm, he reached for the foot and held it in a viselike grip while trying to spin Morton aside. The beast hopped several times as he tried to stomp Tallman's face, but he soon lost his balance and fell.

Tallman scrambled to his feet and turned to face Morton who was already on his knees and holding his nine-inch knife. "I'm gonna cut your fuckin' hands off, mister. And you're gonna watch the whole thing."

"He'll do it too!" someone in the crowd whispered.

But before the whispering onlooker had said three of his four words, Tallman kicked at Morton's hand and sent the knife sailing. While the stunned woman beater was looking at his empty hand, Tallman kicked the still kneeling hulk square in his jaw. A mist of blood and several teeth erupted from Morton's mouth and he fell back. To be sure, Tallman walked forward and dug the heel of his boot into Morton's face until the thug stopped moving. That's when he heard the hammer on a revolver.

Hayward had caught one of Morton's drunken sidekicks going for his gun. But before the rat-faced no-account had cleared leather, Hayward had the glistening blue barrel of his Smith American pressed into the man's temple. "You gonna be next, chicken-shit?" he asked playfully. "Now why don't you just finish taking that rusty Colt out of that beat-up sling and drop it on the floor." Then he turned to the other two. "You. Both of you! Do likewise and be quick about it so the rest of us can get back to enjoyin' the evening."

The crowd roared and the drummer released a short and snappy drumroll topped by a loud hit on his cymbal.

"Now," Hayward added, "why don't you three get your shit-ass boss out of here before I throw up on you. And I ain't kiddin', boys. Now git!" He kicked one in the ass as he staggered toward Morton.

Tallman scooped up Morton's knife as he went toward the bar.

"Whiskey," he said to the barkeep. As he was admiring the finely crafted knife, the saloon girl, still shrugging into her torn dress, approached Tallman.

"I ought to take that knife and cut that bastard's balls off," she said.

"He's got enough trouble," Tallman grunted, still admiring the knife. He'd decided to keep it.

"Anyhow, mister, thanks," the bitter and ragged-looking woman said as she turned to walk off.

"Anytime," Tallman answered.

"It's on the house, mister," the bartender said as he arrived with a fresh bottle of high quality rye. "That son of a bitch has been causing trouble in here for too damn long. Glad someone finally cleaned his ass."

Tallman nodded and drained the whole shot in one gulp. He wondered if he had a broken rib. It sure as hell felt like it. Were it not for a few lucky breaks he might have had to kill the fatman. "Why don't you get a twelve-gauge and shoot the bastard the next time he beats up on your girls?" Tallman asked the barkeep while he was pouring another shot. "All that talk about cuttin' people up is a bunch of wind. Put a load of buckshot in his fat face. From what I seen yesterday it don't seem there's no penalty for shootin' people in Cuero."

The barkeep walked off and left the bottle.

Tallman had never been able to figure why people like Tinker Morton could run roughshod over the fainthearts. While pondering the thought, he remembered that he had two of Aaron Wagner's impact grenades in his pocket. They were on the same side he'd fallen on. He wondered what a mess they might have made if they had gone off.

"Those boys will be workin' half the night to haul their leader back to their camp," Hayward said when he returned to the bar. "That pig has got to go three hundred or better."

"Thanks," Tallman said, his tone sincere.

"No problem, Turk. I'll throw my cards in with any man that's willing to stomp a bastard like Tinker Morton. Especially one that's willin' to do it to save a lady's honor!"

They both laughed because they both knew that it was more than the honor of a saloon girl, much more. It was plain and simple fun to bust the skull of someone like Tinker Morton.

"Nice-lookin' knife you got there, Turk," the neat Hayward said.

"Yeah," Tallman agreed, as he tested the blade on the hairs on the back of his forearm.

"Looks like someone spent some time with the stones," Hayward said as he watched the blade shave cleaner than a barber's razor. "Mind if I have a look?"

"You partial to knives, Frank?" Tallman asked as he handed the blade to Hayward.

"Collector of sorts," Hayward lied, his mind working toward the future.

"Keep it."

"Right nice of you, Turk," he said as he fondled the

handcrafted knife. "You know, Turk, I might be able to use a man like you in a little venture I've got going. Wages ain't bad."

"Oh, yeah?"

"Hundred dollars a night."

Tallman faked a wide-eyed and eager expression. That was three months' wages for most men. Whatever Hayward had going, it was likely to be on the wrong side of the law.

SEVEN

Tallman was sleeping with one eye open. He didn't doubt that Tinker Morton might come back with reinforcements for a second bout.

So he was ready when he heard the ladder to the loft creaking. He quietly drew his Colt, rolled to his stomach, and aimed at the center of the rectangle framed by the uprights and the ladder rungs.

"Jesus Christ!" he groaned when he saw the outline of a woman's head. He'd remembered to lay on the Georgia twang. "A person could get shot creepin' around at this ungodly hour."

At first he didn't recognize her. Then she spoke. "It's me."

"Oh," he sighed.

She climbed the final rungs and stepped through the four-foot opening and into the livery loft. The moon was bright and it backlit her frame in a ghostly manner. She was dressed modestly, her hair had been brushed out, and her war paint had been scrubbed off. He thought she looked more like a farmer's daughter than a saloon girl. But then he mused that she probably had been a farmer's daughter before the lure of the fast life had dragged her away from the land and into the outhouse pit.

"I asked Frank Hayward where you were stayin'."

"He still up and around?" Tallman asked. Hayward and he had spent two more hours at Bank's bar before Hayward decided they ought to visit Maybell's Dance Hall. Tallman had begged off. He never paid for it unless it became unavoidable in the line of duty.

"Hayward is always around," she said as she stepped toward the bedroll. "That's one thing I wanted to tell you about, you bein' so nice to me tonight. Wasn't another man in Bank's that had the backbone to stand up to that bastard."

"Last night's more like it," Tallman said as he motioned for her to sit on a bale of hay. "It must be damn near sunup."

"It's three thirty," she said, her voice as innocent as her looks. "But I just got off work at two and I wanted to soak after being touched by that hog."

"Don't blame you for that," he replied, having earlier washed up in the trough in back of the stable. He'd figured he would get on better with Hayward than if he smelled like a trail hand who'd been in the saddle for a month without a bath. "So what do you have to tell me about Hayward? He don't seem like a bad sort."

"I don't know nothin' for sure," she started slowly. "But several of the girls have said that he gets to talkin' when he's carryin' a load of whiskey. Though he don't say nothin' clear like, he's got some big deal workin'."

"That so?" Tallman said, faking surprise.

"And the deal don't seem legal. At least the girls don't think it's legal."

"Hell," Tallman blurted, brushing the matter aside, "I've only been here two days and I ain't seen much that *was* legal!"

She didn't respond at first. The pair sat quietly in the warm night breeze which moved gently through the loft, stirring the scent of the straw and hay.

"Well, Mr. Willis, I just thought I'd tell you," she said after the momentary silence.

"Hey, now!" Tallman said cheerfully. "Mr. Willis was my daddy. Folks call me Turk." Tallman was pushing forty, but he had the body of a younger man. Hearing her call him Mr. Willis made him feel a might too old. "And what do I call you?" he asked.

"Heather," she said as she got up and walked the eight feet toward his bed of loose straw. "And the warnin' about Hayward isn't the only reason I come here," she continued as she knelt beside him. "You saved me from a sure beatin' tonight. Tinker Morton has already done smashed up two of the girls an' carved his initials in the belly of another with that big knife of his. That son of a bitch was sure to have hurt me bad before the sun come up this mornin'."

"No need for thanks," Tallman said, brushing off her comment casually. "Men like Morton need their teeth kicked in once every couple of weeks." He paused and noticed her clean scent and the childlike look on her face. He reckoned she was shy of twenty years but that she'd likely packed forty years of hard living into that short life. "And I do thank you again for the warning on Frank Hayward. Man needs all the help he can get when he's on the owlhoot. Fact is, I'd appreciate anything more you can find out. Dandy Frank wants to bring me in on his operation, but I ain't got a clue what the hell it's all about."

"Like I was sayin', Turk, I also have another reason for comin'. I come here to thank you proper," she said as she pulled her plain cotton dress over her head.

Tallman's loins stirred when he saw the milk-white breasts in the glow of the moon. He had had no time to appreciate their beauty while he was kicking Tinker Morton's teeth in.

"You don't have to do this," Tallman said. "Truth be known I pleasured in stompin' that pig."

She didn't reply. She stared at him and allowed

him to observe. "Mister . . . I want to do it. Ain't too often I run into a real man." Then she moved her hands up and cupped the twin mounds. "Do you like them?" she asked playfully.

"Don't guess there's a man alive that wouldn't, Heather."

She lay down on his blanket and pulled him down. As she began to undo his shirt her mind was becoming engulfed with her task. She was set on giving Turk Willis everything she had to offer. Ever since she'd run from home at fourteen to escape her stepfather's sexual abuse, no man had cared enough about her to come to her side like Willis had. And she was going to be sure to tell him how much she appreciated it . . . in the only way she knew how.

Once she'd slowly stripped Tallman of his clothing, she squirmed out of her cotton bloomers, revealing a dark brown triangle. Tallman reached between her legs and sunk a finger into her warmth.

"Oooh," she moaned as she shuddered under his touch and began to slowly press her pelvis into his hand.

Tallman lowered his head and gathered a large nipple into his mouth while she gently palmed his balls. Warm slippery fluids began to come from her crack and Tallman probed her cunt until he found her hard clit. The hot love button was as big and as hard as a .68 minié ball.

"Mmmmmm," she groaned as he circled the little knob with his fingertip. "You know how to do a womaaaan." Her pelvis began rising and falling against his hand.

And Tallman's desires were growing with the level of her voice. Her heavy breathing and her animal noises left no doubt about what was to come.

"Aah, Turk," she groaned as she grabbed his head with her free hand and pressed his sucking mouth harder to her breast. She let him go a moment longer and then moved quickly, breaking his hold on her breast and her moist mound. With both hands she grasped his swollen shaft and lowered her head, grabbing the throbbing tip firmly in her mouth. Tallman reached from behind and latched on to her wet lips. Soon his hips were rising rhythmically to meet her sucking as his finger worked her clit.

She grunted as her hips bucked harder against Tallman's hand. Then she released her fluids just as Tallman began to release his.

He let her know she could back off, but she ignored the offer and pumped and sucked him dry. And when she was done, she slowed down . . . but she didn't stop. She was just getting started. Tallman relaxed and felt himself growing again in the grip of her youthful lips.

EIGHT

Vanity of vanities, saith the Preacher, vanity of vanities; all is vanity!' " Vivian chanted at the congregation of the Cuero Baptist Church. Almost to her surprise, Sheridan Garwood had gotten her in to do the guest sermon the Sunday after they'd met.

" 'What profit hath a man of all his labor which he taketh under the sun?' " she asked them, quoting from Ecclesiastes. Of all the Bible reading she'd been forced to do as a child, only Ecclesiastes ever made any sense.

" 'The thing that hath been, it *is that* which shall be; and that which is done *is* that which shall be done: and *there* is no new thing under the sun.' " She was holding the forty or fifty churchgoers in the palm of her hand. But, though she was enjoying the role, the scene left her uneasy. She was shocked that she, a libertine, could so easily lead a flock of believers.

"Praise the Lord!" a man in the back shouted, his hands aloft like those of a frantic buyer at a cattle auction.

A chorus of amen's echoed through the small church.

Sheridan Garwood looked upon the small crude pulpit as if Christ himself had returned to give the sermon. Vivian had taken him by surprise. He was equally fascinated by her command of the Bible and by her womanly charms. His cock was as stiff as an ax handle.

"Ecclesiastes. Chapter twelve. Verses thirteen and fourteen." After that she fell silent and looked about the room. Then she began to read, slowly at first. " 'Let us hear the conclusion of the whole matter: Fear God!' " she shouted. " 'And keep His commandments: for this is the whole duty of man. For only God shall bring every work into judgement, with every secret thing, whether *it* be good, or whether it be evil.' "

Upon hearing her final words, Garwood, at once, thought of his hard-on and crossed his legs as if to obscure God's view.

After eyeing the congregation one final time she backed away and sat down amid a chorus of amen's, Praise the Lord's, and other Christian chants.

The regular pastor of the Cuero Baptist approached the lectern. After a closing hymn and prayer, the long-necked, prune-faced preacher reminded all that the end-of-summer picnic and baptism would begin right after the benediction.

While the members were slowly streaming out the door, the handsome Garwood pounced on Vivian with profuse and trite words of praise, all the while keeping a tender grip on her upper arm which left his manicured fingertips only inches from her breast.

"Truly moving!" he went on. "I've always cherished the words of Ecclesiastes."

"Thank you," Vivian responded with a fake smile. Garwood was a fine chunk of man and she still had more to learn about the Suttons and the Taylors and the thought of that vague task left her with problems.

"What do you say to our going to the picnic together?" he asked. "It would keep you from having to tack up your team."

"Why, Sher! I'd like that!" she answered, looking at the supple, sun-bronzed skin of his face. "Is it far?"

"Several miles south of town. A beautiful cottonwood grove on the Guadalupe River. We've been going there for years to baptize the converts and the youngsters who are ready to accept the Lord."

At his carriage, he helped her up, nearly shuddering openly at her scent and at the thought of what lay beneath the starched and pressed white blouse. The effect the bright sun had on the auburn hair visible under the dark blue bonnet reinforced a feeling that had been growing since he'd met her the Wednesday before: *He had to have this woman for his own.*

During the trip to the picnic site, she sat closer than she had to and attempted to prod Garwood into talking more about his role in the feud. She had sensed Garwood's growing attraction and she was pleased to employ her womanly charms to pry information from the deacon and banker. As he relaxed and spoke more freely, it was obvious that there was more to him than he showed to the public at large. He was a man of vision. He could see that America was about to explode into an era of invention, massive capital accumulation and widespread wealth. And he talked of the West being the breadbasket of America, of the world. But whenever she angled him toward his role as peacemaker in the feud, he'd stray and begin talking of the future of the West. He was full of himself, openly revealing his own lust for power and position.

" 'All is vanity,' " she said playfully, interrupting his explanation of his general plan to acquire land and get a foothold in the cattle business. " 'A vexation of the spirit!' "

"Of course it is, Isabelle," he answered. "But you'll never convince me that the good Lord has anything against wealth as long as it does not become a substitute god. 'Ask and it shall be yours!' "

"True," Vivian agreed. "But I have found that the

love of money may easily overshadow the love of the Lord. We try to avoid it, though we often fail."

"Do you speak from personal experience?" Garwood asked, a devilish smile spread from ear to ear.

"I'm a human being."

Garwood chuckled and urged the horses on with the supple and ornately engraved reins. "You know, we'd make an unbeatable team," he blurted. "I'd watch over the money and you'd watch over my soul and keep the false gods away."

"Then who'd look after my soul?" she said flirtatiously, her eyes revealing a mischievous glitter.

He answered only with a knowing glance.

"There it is," Garwood said. "Pretty place, isn't it?"

Vivian agreed. A grassy area shaded by cottonwoods sloped toward a sandy but narrow beach on the Guadalupe. The high sun glistened on the slow-moving water.

The women were already starting fires and laying colorful linens on the plank and sawhorse tables assembled by the men the night before. Children squealed and hooted as they splashed in the river.

Once Garwood had hitched the team to a low branch on a cottonwood, they made their way to the table which was laid out with a fresh pot of coffee and meticulously arranged china. One of the ladies poured two cups and complimented Vivian on her sermon. "Very appropriate," she said. "You know how the Baptists love to pass judgment on others. Why just last week the Reverend Harper spouted off about the evils of John Barleycorn. Claimed that all who drink are kin to the devil!"

Vivian got wide-eyed. "Strong drink can lead a person astray," she said. "That's a fact."

"Well, you don't see my Henry here do you, Mr. Garwood?"

"No, Nellie, I don't."

"Well, you won't. Said he's all through with churchgoin' since the preacher passed judgment on him and others what likes a drink to take the rough edges off'n life! Says he ain't no kin to the devil."

"I'm sure he's not, ma'am," Vivian added. "We can only pass judgment once we've obtained a Christlike perfection ourselves. And the good Lord knows that there's no such perfection on His earth."

"Hallelujah and amen!" the woman said.

Pleased to be free of Nellie, she and Garwood made the rounds as her escort introduced her to the town's Baptists. She couldn't help notice that the women looked at Garwood with either an evil eye or an adoring eye. There was no in-between. Also, she observed that it was one of the quietest gatherings she'd ever attended. There was no music to promote the devil's dancing and none of the devil's brew to mellow the soul. The women gathered together to talk child rearing and to swap tales of the evildoing of those not present. The men argued church politics. The playful noises made by the children seemed almost sacrilegious.

After only a small dose of it all, Vivian prodded Garwood into taking a walk up the quaint stream.

"The Suttons and Taylors Baptists?" she asked after they'd walked awhile in silence.

"Most are if I recollect right. You seem to have an intense interest in our feud, Isabelle," Garwood went on. "Hardly an hour goes by that you don't bring it up."

Vivian stopped and turned toward the banker, momentarily taken aback. "You'll have to admit that it certainly is something! Why it has become a national curiosity. The New York pulp peddlers are having a field day. They churn out thousands of books each time another shooting takes place. As a Christian missionary, I do admit that the whole thing goes beyond my understanding of humankind."

Garwood was only half-listening. *His* attention was centered on her breasts. Every primitive urge in his being told him to reach out and touch, to hold her in his arms, to feel her soft lips. His cock was straining against his trousers.

Vivian, an expert on men and the nature of their inborn lust and need for instant gratification, sensed his longing and suggested that they return to the picnic.

When they arrived back at the end-of-summer celebration, the reverend was just wading into the slow-moving water, followed by his flock of soon-to-be-dunked recruits to Christianity. They both edged forward for a ringside seat.

Vivian tried to appear interested in the immersions in spite of her disjointed thoughts. There were several tense moments when the preacher's words went on too long and the newly indoctrinated came up sputtering and choking. But for the most part the ceremony was boring and it struck her as absurd. After the last soul had been saved by dunking, the drenched reverend called for a prayer. Once the flock had complied with his wish, he announced that the Sunday evening service would start at seven. Then he reminded them of the Tuesday night Bible class, Wednesday evening service, Thursday's deacons meeting, and the Saturday meeting of the woman's auxiliary.

When the final word had been spoken by the leader of the flock, Garwood angled Vivian toward the wagon. He seemed overly anxious to leave.

"It's a beautiful afternoon," she said as he helped her up. "Let's ride up the river road and then over to Cuero." She was determined to be able to report something to Tallman the next time they met, something more than she'd learned already . . . which was nothing! Her afternoon with Garwood had convinced her that he was something more than a pompous deacon with good looks, a banker, and a feud arbitrator. It was something she saw in his eyes, something beyond his desire to haul down her bloomers.

Garwood headed up river as Vivian had requested. He was pleased to have any reason to prolong his day with Isabelle MacKenzie. But regardless of how hard Vivian tried to get Garwood on the topic of the feud, he always slipped off in other directions. And it seemed unintentional, especially the last time when he began to lament the death of his wife. "She died of cholera only a week before the cannon fired on Fort Sumter," he said, the reins loose in his hands. The pair of chestnuts seemed to know the way as they pulled the expensive carriage effortlessly over the bumpy river road. "It's hard to find a good woman."

"A horrible loss," Vivian added, fully aware of the nature of Garwood's bullshit line. *Time to hang on to my skirt*, she thought to herself.

"It was . . ." He paused. Then after a few seconds of silence, he picked up the reins and pulled the horses to a halt. "I must tell you, Isabelle. I find you overwhelming." Then he encircled her with his arms and kissed her lips, gently at first.

Surprised but not discouraged, she sat quietly as he began probing with his tongue and hands. He wasn't clumsy or unpracticed as he pulled her blouse out of her skirt and pushed his hand up to her breasts. She began to glow under his touch and at once she felt her wetness. Gently, he pulled the cups of her corset downward and released the twin orbs. She returned his probing kiss, offering just enough passion to let Garwood know she had it in her. His kissing became more urgent and he began to unbutton her blouse. When he had her breasts bared to the late August sun, he released her lips and moved his mouth to one of her hard nipples and began to suck gently, and then to circle the large nipple with an expert tongue. Vivian was sorely tempted to take the banker all the way. She ran her fingers through his curly, soft, brown hair and began to become vocal. She wasn't acting.

"Oo, Sher!" She pushed his head firmly onto her breast as his sucking became more feverish.

Then his hand went under her petticoat and quickly he pulled the bloomers aside and began to stroke her. She pushed her pelvis into his hand and held more firmly onto his hair. "Oh, Sher . . . oh, my God!" Then she backed away from his sucking lips and pushed his hand from her throbbing cunt. "God forgive us!" she said aloud, her eyes cast aloft. "It's not right, Sher."

Garwood held onto her breast and fingered the hard nipple.

"No, Sher . . . please!"

"If God didn't want people to enjoy lovemaking, he wouldn't have made us this way," Garwood insisted, still toying with her nipple. His balls were aching as they hadn't in years. He'd had half a hard-on ever since her morning sermon, and his rod had been like a rifle barrel since the walk upstream at the picnic.

Vivian was on the edge herself. But she knew she still had nothing from Garwood and she wanted an ace in the hole even though she'd have to satisfy her own desires alone in the tub when she got back to the Gulf Hotel, a poor substitute for the log that strained against Garwood's trousers.

"Sher," she said gently as she pulled his hand from her large and solid breast. "God had no objection to love, but this is lust. Lust is the work of Satan!"

At first Garwood appeared to have rape in his eyes. Instinct was overshadowing reason. The thing in his pants was screaming for relief. Then he settled back in the carriage seat and looked at the wet spot on his pants. "Damn," he muttered. "I guess I've made a mess of it now."

"Your pants?" she asked playfully.

"That too," he said as he grabbed his cock through his pants. "Mighty powerful force here."

"I understand, Sher," she said as she began to put her breasts back into their cups. She worked slowly

93

and handled them more than she needed to. She smiled inwardly as she saw she was adding to Garwood's frustration. "I understand the lure of the flesh. And it is because I do understand it that I see the danger in it."

When she started to button her blouse, Garwood abruptly picked up the reins and slapped the rumps of his team.

Neither spoke a word all the way to the Gulf.

When they stopped in front of the hotel, she looked at him in a way that held promise for the days ahead and then broke the silence. "I like you very much, Sher. Please don't be a stranger."

He got out and helped her down. "I'll be around. You can bet on it!" he said, holding onto her hand longer than necessary.

From across the street, Nate Gill, Garwood's arch political enemy, noticed the lingering and hand-holding. *Cute*, he thought to himself as he lit up a large cigar. *The Bible lady and that pompous bastard, two of God's finest creatures*, he sneered inwardly. He spit a wad on the plankwalk in front of the stage and telegraph office and then shouted across the street in his best Scottish brogue. "Owt doin' the Lord's work this fine evenin', Sheridan Garwood!"

Garwood dropped Vivian's hand as if it had suddenly turned into a hot coal and glanced across the street. "That bastard," he muttered. "That sawed-off foreigner is a blight on this goddamned town!"

Vivian was both pleased and shocked. It was the first time Garwood had appeared wholly human since the first moment she'd met him. But she was shocked by the venomous ring of his curse. It wasn't the last time she'd hear it!

NINE

"**W**e'll stop here and wait for dark," Hayward commanded. He was still dressed like a dude. "I only work at night. Easier that way, if you boys get my meanin'."

Tallman dismounted and tied his paint off on a low branch so the horse could graze. He noticed that the two characters Hayward had picked up to round out the quartet went right for their saddlebags. Each came up with partially full bottles of cheap whiskey.

The one with rotten gums and black pegs where his teeth ought to be slugged a gulp of whiskey and held the bottle toward Tallman. "Want a pull, Turk?"

Just the smell of the man's breath was enough to make a maggot puke.

Tallman shook his head again and stared at the pig in a way that let the black-tooth know that he could kiss off.

"Some partner you are, Ace. Ain't even partial to drinkin' with friends."

"I ain't had no friends since my granddaddy died, mister," Tallman growled. "And my name ain't Ace."

"All right, you two. Cut the goddamn jawin' and listen up. You can save your nasty natures for the carpetbaggers."

"Carpetbaggers!" grunted the fat one with rotten gums. "You payin' us to get some carpetbaggers? Hell, I'll do that for fun."

"You don't want your twenty dollars?" Hayward asked the loudmouth.

"I'll take his gold," the skinny one said. It was the first time Tallman had heard him speak since they'd met up earlier in the day. "Brownie'd just waste it on some stink-pussy whore."

The fat one named Brownie gave the evil eye to his sidekick but Tallman had already guessed that the skinny one was the cold-blooded killer in the duo. It was in his eyes.

"You'll take shit, Dirk," Brownie snarled.

The gaunt-faced, slender outlaw stared momentarily at his oversized partner and snickered as he squeaked the cork from his bottle.

Tallman rested his hand on the handle of his .45-caliber long Colt. He wondered what one of his explosive-tipped slugs would do to the lean, rat-faced hard case. The man couldn't weigh more than a hundred and ten pounds. The two twenty-dollar outlaws were still locked in a deadly stare, though Tallman had no doubt the lard-assed black-tooth would walk away.

He finally did and Dirk spat.

Hayward had not filled him in on details. But he had explained that he was getting his hundred dollars to keep an eye on Brownie and Dirk. "If they even look like they are going to be trouble," Hayward had warned, "kill 'em!"

"You boys done buttin' heads?" Hayward asked, the tone of his question clear.

Tallman sensed that Frank Hayward could kill the pair as easy as spitting on a rock. It was a side of Hayward he'd not seen until that moment. He made a note to be careful when his back was toward the well-dressed slicker.

"Ain't no call to git nasty, now," Dirk said as he walked toward Tallman and Hayward. "Me an' Brownie's rode together since the war and we ain't tangled yet. Of course we done tangled with plenty of other men, me an' him together, and most of 'em's pushin' up daisies." He turned to the fat one. "Now that's the truth, ain't it, Brownie?"

Brownie laughed.

"Listen up or saddle up," Hayward said.

As Hayward began to explain their mission, the tension subsided. He told them that they were going to hit a Yankee rancher who, using carpetbagger in-fluence, had forced a loyal Rebel off his land. With what appeared to be an honest dislike for northerners, Hayward explained that he was in the employ of a se-cret group of deposed southern officers and political officials who were determined to trouble the Yankees as long as they or their carpetbagger kin were on Texas soil.

"The plan is simple," Hayward went on. "We're going to burn the bastard's barn."

Tallman's heart sank. He lifted his grimy Stetson and reseated it as he looked into the orange western sky, silently cursing Allan Pinkerton for handing him a family feud. After all, what the hell could a person do, short of killing all the feudists in the county? He sighed aloud and fingered a cheap cheroot from his sweat-stained shirt.

"Hey, Turk! What the hell you doin'? Dreamin' about some saloon girl's titties?" Hayward groaned. "Listen up."

Tallman turned and took two steps toward the barn burners. Hayward had sketched a diagram in the dirt.

"We ain't gonna keel us no Yankees?" the surly, black-toothed man asked, his voice ringing with an honest dismay. "Jes some fuckin' cows?"

"There ain't gonna be no people killin'," Hayward told Brownie. "My people want the sons of bitches alive so they can see their prize breeding stock sizzling in the ashes like many a southern family had to do. I'll be the one doing the killing if any of you guns a man . . . unless, of course, you have to."

"Jesus," Tallman said. "Goddamn shame to kill prize stock. Why don't we just open the doors and let out the cows before we burn it?"

"You some kind of Yankee lover?" Brownie grumbled, his words followed by a stream of stink.

Tallman looked at the animal with eyes that could bore holes in the boiler plate of a steam locomotive. "Truth is, mister, I'd sooner see you go up in flames than any backyard milk cow."

The fatman dropped his bottle and went for Tallman, but Hayward had his Smith & Wesson .44 out and in the face of the hired gun before he'd taken a step. The bull stopped cold when he saw the polished and blued eight-inch barrel and the face of the man on the other end of the flashy hogleg.

"There isn't going to be any of this shit while you're on my time. Now simmer down or get the hell out."

"Christ's sake, Brownie," Dirk whined. "Let's burn the barn and go get us some fresh whiskey and a room full of Mex whores. And maybe if you git lucky you'll run into Ace some night on a dark street."

Though the air was thick with tension, the planning continued without further interruption. As Hayward went on, Tallman quickly pondered a solution to his dilemma. Dirk and Brownie were expendable. And he wasn't about to run off and let the trio of arsonists burn up horses and prize breeding stock. A barn owl was worth more on the face of the earth than black-tooth Brownie and the runt, Dirk. This one, he'd decided, would be compliments of the Pinkerton agency . . . no charge.

After the sun had drifted below the horizon, the barn burners mounted up and rode out at a slow trot. For an hour and a half, they rode due south toward Horace Taylor's ranch. Tallman had no idea that the target was Pitkin Taylor's uncle. Horace, well into his fifties when the war started, had fought bravely for the South in three major campaigns and had been decorated on numerous occasions. By the time of the truce, he'd become a two-star general, though there wasn't much left of his command by the time the bluecoats had overrun the South. Taylor was no Yankee sympathizer. Like many southerners he had, in fact, been disenfranchised by the Fourteenth Amendment in 1868.

Hayward slowed his mount and began craning his neck to the right side of the trail. Within several minutes he found what he was looking for and he then dropped from his saddle. In a clump of briars he'd hidden two four-gallon kegs of coal oil.

Tallman took careful stock of the situation. The pair of degenerates were on either side of him and both had their grimy hands resting on their sidearms. And both were watching his every move. Tallman was sure that they had already decided that they'd make buzzard chow of him before the night was out.

Hayward, having recovered the oil, lifted a keg up to one of the twenty-dollar thugs, the skinny one with the loose eye. Then he gave the other keg to Brownie. "Cradle those barrels in your laps. We only got a mile to go."

Once they had crested a smooth, grassy knoll, Tallman could see the faint glow of the farmhouse lamps and the dark outline of the buildings which were lit with a quarter moon. Fully aware that the moment for action was at hand, his senses were heightened. The sounds made by the horses in the still night air seemed unusually loud.

"We'll tie up to those trees," Hayward whispered as he pointed toward a line of trees which created a distinct border between a plowed field and the barnyard. Then he turned to the trio following his tracks. "You boys know your places." He paused for a moment and looked for acknowledgment.

Tallman rubbed his stubble, threw the chewed butt of his cigar into the dirt, and nodded.

Dirk slugged the last of his pint of whiskey and hurled the small bottle over his shoulder. Brownie spat from his dirty, sun-cracked lips, and dismounted.

Hayward circled to the right and the other three

walked straight in from the north. The house was sit-
uated on the south side of the two-hundred-foot,
single-story cow barn. According to Hayward's plan,
they were to pour coal oil along the north wall of the
sprawling barn, light it off in several places and get
out. Hayward was to position himself on the south-
west corner of the building with his Winchester so
that he would be in position to keep the rancher and
his men pinned down in the ranch house and bunk
cabins.

Once Hayward was out of sight on the west side of
the structure, the two twenty-dollar no-accounts
walked toward the barn, each carrying a keg of
kerosene. Tallman was ready. He had one of Aaron
Wagner's spherical grenades in his hand.

"Hey, Brownie," Tallman said when they were
about forty feet from the barn. "Your teeth get like
that from eatin' dog shit?"

When Brownie stopped and spun to face Tallman,
the Pinkerton threw the grenade at the outlaw's feet
as hard as he could. As soon as he'd let fly, he went
for his Colt. But the explosion rocked him back and
off balance.

Brownie was screaming and spinning in the middle
of the fireball.

Tallman saw a muzzle flash beyond the flaming
corpse. He heard the slug before the thump of the
muzzle blast. Instinctively, he dove for the dirt and

drew. Dirk was lit up by the fire that was consuming his sidekick. While the skinny killer fired another angry shot, Tallman quickly but carefully thumbed the hammer on his Colt and fired three even and methodical shots into Dirk's shirt, each of which seemed to lift the little man to his toes. Then his knees gave out.

As he watched his crumbling victim, Hayward rode by at a full gallop shouting at the top of his lungs.

"You don't gun a Sutton! You don't gun a Sutton without paying the price!"

When he rounded the corner, Hayward hesitated after pulling his horse up. "Willis! You son of a bitch!" He was going for his gun as Tallman was scrambling to his feet but he changed his mind when all hell broke loose at his back. Men were pouring from the bunk cabins, firing blindly into the still night air. Hayward kicked his horse and continued his chant. His words were soon overcome by a torrent of gunfire.

Tallman ran the twenty yards to his horse. Though he still had the cover of the barn, he'd be a sitting duck as soon as the angry ranch hands rounded the corner of the building. He jumped on his paint and simultaneously ripped the reins from the small branch. When he heard lead thunking into the branches and the trunks of the larger trees, he hugged the horse's neck and spurred the skittish animal on. He topped the knoll without taking a hit, but he didn't slow down. A small army'd be on his heels in no time. Now out of the range of the ranchers' guns, he had a moment to curse himself for not picking up on the fact that Hayward was, in fact, a feudist. The mistake had cost him his cover, and if the raggedy paint broke down in the next hour, it might cost him his hide.

TEN

Vivian sat alone in the spartan dining room of the Gulf Hotel. She was reading the front page of *The DeWitt County Democrat* with some trepidation. The feature story was the grisly tale of a foiled barn burning at Horace Taylor's spread. Three pen and ink drawings, a burned corpse, a barn, and bust of Bill Sutton, filled a quarter of the page. The newspaper scribbler had paid particular attention to detail in describing the fried body, including the odd wounds which "seemed to have been inflicted by some small explosive device, something like a small artillery shell." The local rag had concluded that Bill Sutton had been the architect of the failed raid even though he had denied it.

Vivian slapped the four-page daily shut and composed herself. She was trying to convince herself that the burnt body wasn't her partner. But she had a vivid recollection of Aaron Wagner's grenade demonstration.

She was about to get up to make another trip to the telegraph office to see if she'd gotten an answer to her wire to Lockhart when Nate Gill appeared at her table. "Well, Miss MacKenzie," he said in his thick Scottish brogue. "I see your friend, Sheridan Garwood, has left you alone for lunch."

"Do I know you, sir?"

"I'd say not, Miss MacKenzie," he allowed as he doffed his small hat. "But we'll correct that this very moment. Nathan Gill's the name." The Scotsman sat down boldly as he introduced himself.

Garwood headed up a faction of do-gooders that saw Cuero as a *clean* little town which serviced the farmers and ranchers. On several occasions they had tried to pass ordinances against the public display of sidearms, the consumption of whiskey and beer, whorehouses, and, to use their words, "other displays of human decadence."

Gill, on the other hand, thought it absurd to run off the free-spending cattle drovers, hard-drinking ranch hands, peddlers, drifters, and other no-accounts who might want a game of billiards, a bottle of firewater, or a five-dollar look-see at one of Maybell's dance hall girls. His reasons were obvious.

"May I buy you lunch, Miss MacKenzie?" he asked.

Vivian, the telegraph office weighing heavily on her mind, was about to refuse. But she had intended to visit Gill's sooner or later, and this gave her the perfect in. Anyhow, she'd decided shortly after she met Tallman that he was indestructible. And she would find it interesting to learn more about the governor's number-one DeWitt County political enemy.

"Is it that time of the day already?" she asked.

"Just shy of one o'clock."

"I'd enjoy something light."

"My pleasure then," the five-and-a-half-foot Scotsman chimed in. "The Gulf isn't much to look at. But I insist on her being clean and serving good food."

"You own the Gulf?" she said, faking surprise.

"Yes, I do. And she's one of the few in southeast Texas with tubs in the rooms."

Vivian was immediately amused by the lively, red-faced Scotsman. His outward appearance was that of a harmless whiskey drummer who always had the latest string of dirty jokes and who always consumed too many free samples, the kind of man who would plunk down his last four silver dollars to buy a round of drinks for a bunch of strangers. But there was more to Nate Gill than met the eye. A man didn't end up owning a third of a town by being a stumblebum.

"Pretty vivid stuff," Gill said, nodding toward the newspaper.

"The Devil's work, Mr. Gill. And that's a fact."

"The way it has been going, the Devil will be the only one left in the County," Gill said. He didn't seem upset. "The Suttons and the Taylors and all their damn-fool followers will likely kill each other off before Christmas."

After a few more minutes of small talk, a waiter came over to the table and paid great deference to Nathan Gill and Isabelle MacKenzie. Gill ordered a small steak for each of them and added a double scotch whiskey to his own order. "I hope you are not offended."

"I have no objection to the moderate consumption of spirits," she said. "Nowhere in my Bible does it outlaw the pleasures of grain or grape." As she spoke, she did so in a way which might lead Gill to suspect that her Bible operation might be a con game. Her knowing smiles, the glow in her eyes, and the timbre of her voice revealed bits and pieces that a suspicious man like Gill might latch on to. He obviously had some reason for inviting her to lunch.

As they waited, she easily moved the conversation to the feud. Rumor had it that Pitkin Taylor had taken a turn for the worse and was not expected to live.

Like Garwood, Gill seemed indifferent as to which family might come out on top. Both had written it off quickly as a wasteful folly. However, unlike Garwood, Gill expressed an interest in the business prospects.

He bluntly explained that he cared not one whit that the warring factions might kill each other off.

"I'm not much on the Gospel," Gill added. "But I do know there is some force out there. I call it Mother Nature. And the way I see it, Mother Nature is doing her damnedest to rid the county of fools and idiots. And more power to her!"

"Harsh words, Mr. Gill."

"Harsh but true, Miss MacKenzie," he said as he raised his glass. Then he took a large gulp. "And once they're gone, some fine ranchland will be on the auction block for a fraction of its value. And you'll see me in the front row with a sack of banknotes."

Vivian was taken with the aura of unchecked ambition which suddenly shrouded the ruddy Scotsman. She began to wonder. It was the same thing she'd seen in Garwood.

ELEVEN

Tallman had ridden hard all night, though he'd never heard any horses on his trail. Just as the eastern sky had turned a dull blue, he had traded his horse for a big-boned gray which he'd found standing quietly in a small paddock behind a ramshackle barn. He'd felt bad about taking the farmer's only horse. But he had felt worse about the possibility of being guest of honor at a frontier necktie party.

At ten o'clock he had crossed the Guadalupe and had ridden an infrequently traveled path which ran parallel to Plum Creek. All the while he had tried to make sense out of the attempted barn burning. Why hadn't Frank Hayward declared his Sutton allegiance? Doing so would have been no big surprise to anyone in DeWitt County.

Ten miles south of Lockhart, Tallman happened upon a small pond created by a sharp bend in the creek. The early afternoon sun had drenched his clothing with sweat, accenting his sorry appearance and odor. He grunted and pondered Vivian's more civilized role. He imagined that she was, at that moment, enjoying dinner in one of Cuero's eateries, a dinner she had likely conned out of some flapjaw Christian do-gooder.

The still pool looked inviting so he pulled up the well-mannered gray and dismounted. In moments he'd undressed and thrown his clothing into a clump of bushes. He flopped into the warm water and immediately began to feel revived as layers of grime washed away. While reviewing the events of the past week, he recalled an idea which had crossed his mind during the governor's briefing. It was an idea that might get him into the homes of both the Suttons and the Taylors. His mood elevated by the possibilities, he dried himself quickly, shaved, and put on a set of fresh duds he had stowed in his saddlebags. Then he set the gray in a fast walk for Lockhart.

Outside of town, he dismounted, stripped the friendly horse of his tack, and gave the beast a slap on the rump. At once, the heavyset horse set down the trail they'd just ridden. Tallman hoped the kindly gray would find its way back to its owner. He wanted nothing to do with a stolen horse.

With his gear over his shoulder, he walked the last mile into Lockhart.

"Goddamned rattler spooked my horse and the poor devil stepped in a gopher hole and broke her right hind," Tallman told the old man tending the Lockhart Livery. "Had to put her down. And it wasn't easy. That mare had been a damned good companion."

The withered old-timer grunted and spat a stream of tobacco juice that would have doused a campfire. "Yep," he grunted as he put Tallman's saddle on a rack in the tackroom.

"How much do I owe you?"

"Two bits a day to keep your stuff. You want another horse and you got to wait until Mr. Middleton gets here. He does the tradin'."

"Here's four dollars. I ain't sure what I want to do. Might just stay on and have a look at your town."

The old man spat again, leaving a huge mark in the dust. "Yep." Then he walked off.

Three doors up from the livery, Tallman found a four-bit hotel and took a room. "Bath and women's extra," the clerk explained as Tallman took his key and saddlebags and moved toward the front door. After a ten-minute walk toward the center of town, he saw the store he had been looking for. It had the biggest display window in Lockhart, a touch of New York in dusty Texas. The well-dressed dummies he'd seen in the window during their earlier visit had caught his eye. And the store's sign stood out like a whore in church. Two feet by fifteen feet, it announced Gold's Fine Clothing—gold leaf on a glossy black background.

It didn't take him long. He knew exactly what he wanted and within a half hour, he was on his way back to the third-rate hotel.

When he reached his room, he dumped the armload of packages on the bed and stood back, satisfied with his new approach to the Sutton-Taylor mess. He was about to become Henry Ravensdale, a New Yorker, and a writer of dime novels about the savage West.

Over the years as one of Allan Pinkerton's most effective—and most unruly—undercover agents, he had become a master of disguise and a self-taught actor. In his days as a Union Army operative in the South, he'd been forced to quickly master numerous roles. He'd posed as the son of a wealthy plantation owner who was making grain deals for the Rebel troops, a war correspondent, a slave catcher, a Florida cattle dealer, a Reb infantryman and even a preacher. And now, a dime-store novelist.

With the aid of a rinse he had in his bags, he changed his sandy hair to a dark black. Though he usually parted it on the side, he took advantage of a natural center part he had and combed it over his ears and then straight back. He attached a black mustache to his upper lip with spirit gum and went to the packages on the bed. He unwrapped the clothing and laid it out. He decided on the dark beige suit, and light yellow shirt with a white collar. Clothed except for his jacket he took his cross-draw rig from the saddle-bags, shrugged into the wet-molded leather apparatus and tied the bottom of the holster to his belt with a leather thong. He emptied his Colt .45 and dropped it on the bed. Then he unwrapped the oilcloth around his .41 Colt New Line, loaded it with five of Wagner's deadly shells and jammed it into the holster, where it rested snugly, held in place with carefully designed and positioned pieces of spring steel which Wagner had sewn into the leather. The three and a half inch barrel and the sleek grips made it the perfect under-cover piece. It was hidden as easily as many small-caliber vest guns, yet it packed the wallop of a large handgun.

He wrapped his long Colt in the oilcloth and stowed it in the new suitcase he'd bought at Gold's. Finally he retrieved his .41 Remington derringer and forearm holster, another of Wagner's inventions. Once he had strapped the quick-release derringer to his arm, he put on his beige jacket and put two spher-ical grenades in his pocket.

Satisfied with his appearance, he put the second new suit, the new shirts, and his other clothing in his new suit bag and snapped the brass latches closed. He then finished tying the brown bow tie and walked to the mirror. He pressed his forearm to his side. With an inaudible click, the latch released the derringer, causing it to fall into the palm of his hand. He quickly raised the tiny gun to the mirror.

"Well, Henry," he said as he stared down the barrels of the derringer. "We're off to end the feud." With that, he chuckled aloud, again taken with the vague nature of the assignment. He was beginning to think that Pinkerton might just as well have sent him off to stop the Civil War in 1861.

After sneaking out the back of the hotel, Tallman made his way through the alleyways for two blocks and emerged on Main Street. The Longhorn was across town on the west side. When he saw the red-lettered sign hanging under a pair of polished horns, he picked up the pace.

"Best room in the house," Tallman commanded of the clerk.

"That would be second floor, overlooking the street. Bedroom and a small sitting room."

"Sold," Tallman said at once, his mood cheerful.

The clerk slid the register around and handed the black-haired city slicker a full pen.

"Mr. Bentham!" the clerk exclaimed when he saw Tallman sign the code name he had given Vivian. "I'd say you are a popular man."

"Oh?"

"I've got two telegrams for you. One came through

yesterday and the other about a half hour ago. About three, I reckon." The helpful clerk turned and fingered two sealed envelopes from one of the cubbyholes and handed them to Tallman. "There you go, Mr. Bentham."

Tallman nodded and left a handsome tip, insisting that he would carry his own bag.

Once in the well-appointed quarters, he dropped the bag and opened the most recent telegram. It was short and to the point: "ARE YOU ALL RIGHT. I.M." Tallman felt good. It was nice to have another human being who cared whether you lived or died. Since his folks had died and until he'd met Vivian, there wasn't a soul who gave a rat's ass but Pinkerton, and his concern was strictly professional.

The other telegram was longer, and was from Allan Pinkerton. Pinkerton rarely contacted his undercover agents in the middle of a case, but this was vital to the operation. John Wesley Hardin, the cousin to Jim Taylor who'd taken part in the Bank's shooting, had killed two Pinkerton agents in a chance encounter on a train eastbound from Houston. Tallman knew both agents. Buck Kingsford and Michael Hart were good men but never as careful as he'd figured they ought to have been. Both had had too much bravado and too few brains. He shook his head and dropped the paper on the expensive bed covering.

All things considered, he felt a bit better about the

Sutton-Taylor case having read the telegram. Though it was no pleasure to hear that two of your colleagues had gone toes up, he at least had something specific to hang his hat on. Pinkerton had assigned top priority to Hardin's capture and ordered him and Vivian to pursue the matter as part of their ongoing investigation. "SEE YOU BACK IN CHICAGO WHEN HARDIN IS IN JAIL," Pinkerton's telegram ended. Tallman got the message. They weren't to return until Hardin had been locked up.

For a moment, he debated a meal or a turn on the goose down. He stripped off his new clothes, laid them on the chair and fell into bed. It wasn't much of a debate. But as he settled into the soft bed, sleep didn't come right away. His mind again settled on Frank Hayward's approach to feuding. It made no sense, and Hayward wasn't a nonsensical man.

TWELVE

Vivian tipped the Mexican boy a quarter after he handed her the sealed telegram. She opened it and read carefully:

ISABELLE MACKENZIE.
GULF HOTEL.
CUERO.
TEXAS.
P INFORMS TWO MISSIONARIES KILLED IN ENCOUNTER WITH OUTLAW. P DECLARES THAT MISSION COMMANDS HIGHEST PRIORITY. MUST SAVE MORE SOULS.

SEE YOU SOON.

A. T.

She folded the yellow paper and glanced down at the morning *DeWitt County Democrat* which lay doubled over next to her coffee cup. She'd just finished reading the front-page story about the railway car shoot-out and was about to start on the piece about Pitkin Taylor's death when the message had arrived. She opened the rag for another look at the headlines: JOHN WESLEY HARDIN GUNS PINKERTONS. Then in a subhead: *Taylor Henchman Adds Two to Count*. She took a sip of coffee, but it had cooled and it tasted foul.

"How fortunate!" Garwood said as he looked down on a pensive Isabelle MacKenzie.

"Oh . . . hello," she said, startled.

"I thought I'd find you here. I wanted to talk to you."

"Please sit down, Sher," she said pleasantly. She welcomed his appearance as she had nothing else to do and she was beginning to wonder what people would think of her failure to hawk Bibles on street corners. Surely they would expect her to preach and pass the plate or to move on to the next town.

"I see you have been reading about Satan's latest deeds in our fine scandal sheet," Garwood said, his face a sheepish mask. He suddenly realized that the feudists didn't have a monopoly on sin. "God knows what will come of it," he added, hoping to recover from his condemnation.

Vivian cocked her head, raised her eyebrows

slightly, and fixed her eyes on the banker in a sideways stare. "The Devil's work is *every*where," she said. "We've all been snagged by his venomous fangs. 'Then Jesus said unto them, I go my way, and ye shall seek me, and shall die in your sins: whither I go, ye cannot come.' John, eight, twenty-one."

"I'd hardly put murder in the same category as the desires of the flesh, Isabelle." He paused and smiled. "God must have had something in mind when he put a fine-looking woman like you on the face of His earth. Frankly, you're a certain pleasure to a man's eyes."

"I thank you for the compliment," she said, now sensing that Garwood's attraction toward her had gone further than lust.

Then he lowered his voice to a sincere tone. "Fact is, Isabelle, I've come to apologize for my indiscretion. I know it was an offense to your faith."

"What about *your* faith, Sher?"

Garwood looked like a tomcat about to pounce on an unsuspecting dove, but he didn't answer. "And . . ." He paused purposefully. "And . . . I want to show my appreciation by asking you to accompany me on a picnic outing this noon."

"Another church affair?"

"Not likely," he said, his voice almost scornful.

"Why not?" She had no other plans and it was better than begging for coin on the street corner, a part of her undercover scheme which she'd been able to avoid thus far. With Tallman on his way back to Cuero and the demise of the two Pinkertons, she guessed that they would be taking a new approach to the case. She wondered if this invitation might not be the last one she'd have. With the pompous façade slowly falling away, she somehow sensed that she might learn something, especially if she pushed him to the limit. In any event she doubted that she could resist the huge lump in his trousers one more time.

"My housekeeper, Teresa, packed a real feast."

"Lead the way," she said cheerfully. She felt good, sure that the layer of sniffish deaconism Governor Trowbridge had complained of was slowly being stripped away, like the skin of a molting rattlesnake.

When they emerged from the Gulf, Vivian noticed that they had another perfect day. The air was warm but dry. Cotton ball clouds drifted on a gentle breeze. She was charged with energy and determined to have something to report to Tallman when he returned.

Once they were under way in Garwood's fancy carriage, he explained that he knew of a spot five miles up Sandies Creek. "Secluded spot" were his words.

Vivian chuckled aloud when she looked out of the corner of her eye and saw the state of his left trouser leg.

"What?" he asked.

"Oh, nothing," she insisted as she put her hand on his forearm. "Just such a beautiful day. And I was momentarily amused at how easy it is to forget how nice it can be to drop everything and simply consume some of God's beautiful handiwork, even that little bit He put here in Texas." She'd decided to capitalize on his boyish intentions. "Sometimes I wish I could drop the ministry and settle down. I once saw a beautiful spot northwest of Canon City, Colorado. Right on Cottonwood Creek. Don't know why it sticks in my mind." Then she sighed and removed her hand.

It was then that Garwood began rambling about settling down. At least it appeared like rambling now that his words were not all measured and accented with Baptist jargon about the evils of humanity.

"I'd like to raise a family," he droned on as he pulled the matched chestnuts off the two-rut road and directed them across a hundred yards of brown grass toward a line of trees. "Never got to it before my first wife died. But now that I'm settled I can provide anything a woman and children could ask for." He turned to her with an intense look on his bronzed, sharp features. "No woman though."

"Why, Sher!" Vivian exclaimed. "Seems to me that a handsome gent like you could lure some fine Baptist lady into the bonds of matrimony."

"Here we are," he said as if he hadn't heard her. He pulled up to the stream's edge and stopped.

"Why it *is* beautiful," she agreed.

"Jim Taylor's land."

Her senses were jolted slightly. "One of the feudists?"

"One of the principal ones!" Garwood answered sounding more like a proud father speaking of a son than a deacon speaking of murder and human chaos.

"Well, it is pretty. Wouldn't it be a beautiful spot for a ranch house?"

"That it would," he agreed, his eyes flashing an odd glitter. "And if the fools don't settle this feud, I'll own it."

Vivian saw that look again. "You?" she responded with surprise, part fake, part real. She was a bit taken with his self-assured pronouncement. "What would you do with grasslands?"

"Raise cows," he said as he bounded out of his wagon. "Nothing says I've got to rust away in a dingy old bank for the rest of my life just because I own sixty percent of the stock. This country is growing, Isabelle. And it runs on beef," he went on, sounding like a politician speaking to the Cuero Merchants Association. "A man with the right backing could become richer than King Midas in the beef business. Most ranchers are small-timers. Most are forced to sell regardless of price, always pressed with current expenses, especially those with large notes on their land. Wasn't much left after the war and just about everybody had to start up on borrowed money." He paused and allowed Vivian an ear-to-ear grin. "I should know. Most of them in DeWitt County do business at my bank."

"It all sounds so futuristic," she said, swooning over his speech. "But I sure don't understand how you are going to get Mr. Taylor's ranch."

Garwood scrambled playfully around the carriage and helped her down. "Simple. He's already three months back," he said as he took her hand. All his sniffish air had vanished. "And I can't let it go much further," he snickered like a kid plotting to rob the melon patch. "Bank policy."

Sheridan Garwood, Peacemaker, she thought to herself, trying hard to hold her girlish smile.

"And *you're* bank policy," Vivian added. Her interest in the man was soaring. The greedy twinkle in his eye spoke for itself.

He suggested that they lay out the lunch and blanket and then take a short walk upstream.

She watched as the tall, square-shouldered deacon set out the blanket and lunch basket. He was nimble and energetic as he went about his task. She wondered if the hard thing in his shorts was still there. Something told her she was going to find out before the afternoon was up.

As they started up the small stream, Vivian pushed back the blue bonnet, undid the plain silver clip holding her long, auburn hair, and shook the silky mass free. She saw Garwood looking and smiled inwardly, suspecting that his manhood was likely swollen with desire. She'd played him pretty hard and had decided to push him further. As they walked and chatted, she frequently touched his arm and, on several occasions, bumped him with her breast. And little by little she dropped the idea that the ministry was providing a mounting frustration rather than an ongoing source of joy.

After only a short time, they turned and headed back toward the buggy.

"I've started to feel as if I've done my share," she said as she approached the blanket. "The good Lord knows how many Bibles I have placed and how much money I have raised for the mission in St. Louis."

Garwood mumbled something, took off his coat and threw it over the carriage seat, then lowered himself on the blanket. Just as she took up a spot on the opposite corner, he opened the basket. A full bottle of French brandy came into full view. The jug dwarfed the sandwiches wrapped in calico napkins.

"A Baptist with a bottle," she said, feigning disgust. "Mercy!"

"One of the church rules which everyone talks about and only a few observe. And I have no doubt that those who abstain simply can't stand the taste of strong drink," Garwood said bluntly. "Damn near enough to make a man become a Roman Catholic."

Vivian laughed and tucked her legs underneath her skirt.

"Will you have a small glass?" he asked hopefully.

"Yes, I will," she said quickly. "I'm not Baptist."

Garwood grunted and poured two ample portions of the amber fluid.

"Isabelle," Garwood blurted after three good portions of the smooth brandy, "I must tell you that . . ." He couldn't spit it out.

"What, Sher?"

"Damn it! I enjoy your company," he said, his mind aflame with his recollection of her breast and the dampness of her slit.

"Why, Sher. I assure you that the feeling is mutual."

"No," he said as he took her hand and pulled her down to the blanket. "More than that."

"Well . . . I . . . don't . . ." she stammered as he lowered his warm lips on to hers.

The lingering kiss was gentle even though it was obvious to her that he was on the edge and about to fall. It had been four weeks since she had held a man's cock in her hand and that was about twenty-six days too long from her perspective. She was as ready as Garwood.

"Oh, Sher," she groaned as she gently pushed him off. "I must contain myself."

But Garwood was not going to give up. Just the animal look in his glowing eyes caused her juices to seep into her cotton panties. The banker put his hand under her slender neck and kissed her again with a rapidly growing urgency. His other hand greedily kneaded her breasts through the starched, white blouse.

"Oooh, mmm. I shouldn't," she moaned as she staged a halfhearted protest.

"I've wanted you since the first moment you stepped into my office," Garwood said after he backed off. "No woman's made me feel the urge as you have, Isabelle."

"We shouldn't," she protested weakly as he knelt upright and methodically undid the buttons on her blouse. Then he untied the bow holding her cups together and gently pulled a breast free, all the while staring into her hazel eyes.

The warm sun added to her lust and she slowly moved her hand to the lump in his trousers. As she held his cock through the fabric of his pants, she brought her legs up and let them fall apart. Garwood instantly palmed her wet cunt as she began to push against his fingers while he sucked a pink nipple deep into his mouth.

Then he stopped and quickly stripped her of her

clothes. When he saw her auburn patch and the swollen lips of her womanhood, he stopped to stare. All men who saw Vivian poised to receive a man were taken speechless by the sight.

"Sher. Hurry," she said as she spread her legs and felt her wetness with her own long fingers. "You can't leave me like this."

Garwood literally ripped his clothing away as he saw her fingering herself. He quickly knelt between her legs and leaned forward to suck her breast once more. Her tits fascinated him. There was nothing to compare with this woman, he thought to himself, not even the pastor's wife. And that was saying something.

"Fuck me, Sher," she said in a raspy voice as she found his meat with her slender fingers. "God, it's so big," she said as she squeezed the thick cock in her hand.

He released her breast, grabbed her thighs, and hoisted her legs to his shoulders. Then slowly, with her guidance, he lowered his turgid prick into her. He shuddered as the warmth engulfed his manhood. His square shoulders loomed large over her as he pushed in and out with slow, careful movements. Then suddenly he leaned forward and plunged into her with a ferocious thrust. Then out slowly. Then another blow.

Garwood's thrusting and grunting was intensifying and another force had him in its grip. Vivian grabbed his balls from behind and held them firmly as she bucked up to meet his animal blows.

Vivian grunted as she massaged his balls and began to convulse. Garwood grunted and began pumping her full of his hot seed. The explosive spurts fueled her own release and her own juices mixed with his and cascaded from her. Though Garwood had finished, he was still hard and he continued to pound her pink opening.

Vivian smiled inwardly. It had been too long.

THIRTEEN

Tallman drove southeast toward Cuero under a blanket of dark-bottomed clouds. He was pleased with his getup and his fine carriage as he moved comfortably in and out of the sun. But the message he'd gotten from the governor troubled him.

In an exchange of telegrams earlier that morning, Trowbridge had explained that Lem Davis, the undercover Ranger, had reported big trouble brewing in the feud. But that wasn't what troubled Tallman. He didn't care if all the feudists in DeWitt County blew themselves to hell. But he did care that Trowbridge had revealed his cover to the Ranger and to the other members of his staff in the statehouse. He'd have to be more careful than he'd planned.

Since the matched pair of gray geldings had been at a slow trot for a while, he hauled them in to a snappy walk. When he made his grand entrance, he wanted the beautiful horses looking fresh. If they were matted with salty sweat they'd contrast poorly to the spiffy carriage with its glossy, highly waxed finish. It was a dark green and the wheels had cream-colored spokes and black rims decorated with white pinstriping. It was sprung for a soft ride and outfitted with highly oiled mahogany tack and polished hammered brass fittings. The collapsible top, which he'd left up, was made of a fine, oiled canvas. It was surely the type of rig a well-to-do New York dandy would drive. Most of all it would attract attention.

When he saw Cuero in the distance it only heightened his concern over the governor's breach of security. He doubted that the first Ranger had been killed by chance. You don't get tied to a tree and shot in the forehead as a result of some random encounter. The man had been executed. And the method was a warning to anyone who had sense enough to see it.

He came into town from the north, and where the twin ruts in the prairie turned into DeWitt Street, he urged the matched grays into a slow, highly organized trot. As he'd expected, the rig and the stunning horses turned all heads. He passed the dry goods store, the Gulf Hotel on the left and headed straight for the livery at the south end of the street.

But when he passed Nate Gill's real estate office,

he heard Isabelle MacKenzie, agent of the Lord. Beyond Bank's, he saw her and her carriage in the vacant lot between Bank's and the Red Dog. Maybell's was right across the street and several of Maybell's girls were perched on the second floor balcony watching the preacher lady. Ten or twelve onlookers were listening quietly.

Amused, he stopped the rig for a look.

"You, sir," Vivian called to the black-haired dandy in the flashy wagon. "You look like a travelin' man. Have you the Good Book to comfort you on your journey lest it end in Hell?"

Tallman, at first partly concealed by the tan-colored top of his rig, leaned further out, smiled, tipped his hat and nodded. He was sure she hadn't recognized him. "Can't say I do, miss," he said with a heavy New York City accent.

She stepped dramatically from her little platform, took a Bible from her inventory and strode toward his carriage. "Why—you—" she stammered before catching herself. "You, sir," she went on loudly as she handed him the Good Book, "you, sir, will need the word to keep you from the Devil's ways. I assure you, it will be a comfort."

"Thank you, ma'am," he said.

"Most folks feel compelled to make an offering to the Lord," she said bluntly.

He looked straight into her eyes and handed her a coin. "Here's a nickel," he said loudly with a nasty expression under his fake black mustache. Then he dropped the coin into her hand in a way that let all the onlookers see the stingy donation.

"Five cents for the Lord's word!" Vivian shouted. "Blasphemy!"

Tallman offered a sarcastic grin and snapped the reins to urge his flashy pair toward the livery.

After putting up his horses and carriage at the livery where he'd slept only three nights earlier, he set out toward the Gulf with his new leather bag.

"Good afternoon, sir," Tallman said to the desk clerk as he strode across the lobby. "I'd like a room. Best in the house, *please*. I'm not used to such crude accommodations."

"Rooms are 'bout all the same," the clerk said with a note of apology in his voice. He looked sorry that he couldn't do better for the flashy stranger who obviously demanded respect. "Do have runnin' water and a tub in the rooms on the first two floors. Only hotel in these parts that does."

"I'll take a room with a tub," Tallman said with a sign of distress.

The clerk slid a dog-eared register toward the dressed-up slicker and then slapped a brass key marked 206 next to the check-in book.

Henry Ravensdale, Tallman signed, in long, slanted, sharp strokes.

"Here on business?" the clerk pried. Oftentimes he could sell information to local merchants for a dollar or two. And he was curious as to why a dude like Ravensdale would set foot in Cuero, Texas.

"That I am!" Tallman responded proudly. "I hope to put this town in the history books."

"How's that?"

"My publisher has sent me here to do the definitive book on the Sutton-Taylor feud, record the events as they unfold."

"Well, ain't that somethin', Mr. Ravensdale."

"Sure is. Folks back East are thirsty for details. The Suttons and the Taylors have become damn near as famous as the Hatfields and the McCoys!"

"You wrote many books?" the clerk asked, eager to know more.

"Quite a number. Mostly about the raw events that are shaping the new West," Tallman obliged the clerk. He wanted the word out and he figured everyone in Cuero would know about him by sundown if he fed the clerk with details.

"You know," the clerk said, "I think I might've read one."

Tallman smiled and nodded, amused that the man had read a book he'd never written. With that, he picked up his bag and headed for the plain, wooden stairs.

It was after midnight before Tallman rapped lightly on Vivian's door.

"I've been wondering when you'd show," she said as she quickly pulled the solid but plain door open.

"Didn't recognize the dandy in the sporty carriage, did you?" he teased after she had closed the door and turned to face him.

"Why, hell! Your own mother wouldn't have known you the way you've got yourself all slicked up like a peacock. You looked like royalty up there on that pretty wagon."

"Royalty? Not this time. But it's an idea I'll have to keep in mind," he said as he pulled an expensive cheroot from his beige vest. "Henry Ravensdale, New York. I'm here in Cuero to write the saga of the Sutton-Taylor feud for a well known New York publisher who wishes to remain anonymous until publication."

"Not bad," she said as she walked to the bed.

Tallman's attention was once again drawn to the hips that moved under the white silk robe. He smiled, knowing that she was moving them a little extra for him. "My feelings too," he agreed finally. "What better way to find out what the hell is going on than to ask the principals."

"You won't be talking to the elder Taylor," she said as she sat down.

He saw that she had the pink nightie on under the white silk. His cock grew slightly and began to throb gently. "I'm aware of that," he said, his tone becoming more serious. He lit the thin cigar and thought of the governor's telegram. His sex urge was replaced with the desire to kick Trowbridge in the ass.

Vivian saw the look. "Troubles," she asked. "I can read that look on your face."

"Trowbridge breached our security agreement. He's informed his undercover Ranger, Lem Davis, that two Pinkertons are also undercover. He didn't give details or reveal our identities. He's also spilled the beans to his staff in Austin."

"Are you still convinced the man's got a Judas in his camp?"

"I'd lay good money on it."

"So we sleep with one eye open and one hand on little Miss Remington," she said, hiking her gown up and tapping the .41 derringer strapped to her milky thigh.

Tallman sighed and took a long pull on his cigar. The sight of her legs and a glimpse of a tuft of hair caused him to wonder out loud: "Miss Valentine, there are times when I think I should have turned you over to the New York authorities."

She snickered and dropped her pink gown and white robe.

"Drink?" she asked.

Tallman insisted and she poured. He went on to explain that Trowbridge was losing patience and that Davis had informed him that the county was about to explode.

"So what are we supposed to do? Work with Davis?"

"No. But Trowbridge wants us to contact him so he can use us for information." He swallowed a gulp of the smooth sour mash. "And I don't like it. I'm still contemplating breaking that son of a bitch's arm next time we meet."

"How do we make contact?"

"You'll enjoy this one. On the walls of the shithouse behind Bank's. I'm supposed to understand the message when I see it."

Vivian laughed at the idea of cryptic messages on the outhouse wall.

"What's so humorous about that?"

Tallman joined in and the pair had a good laugh and then two more drinks before settling down.

"So what have you learned, Bible lady?" he asked, trying to get them back on track.

"Nothing specific. But I have some ideas."

"I'm especially interested in a Frank Hayward. He led the raid on Horace Taylor's spread. Claimed that he was with renegade Rebels who were still at war with the Yankees," he said as he took a pull on his cheroot. "And I believed him."

"I have to admit that it gave me a start when I saw the newspaper. They said one man was burned beyond recognition and partly blown up."

Tallman grinned and sipped his whiskey.

"I do remember Hayward," she said. "He gave me a hard time during my first sermon . . . the day Sutton was shot in Bank's. But I haven't seen him since."

"I wonder if we will. All he knows is that a hard-case somewhere named Turk Willis fouled up his plans. I assume now that he is working for Sutton and I wouldn't want to shake him up, worry him into thinking someone's got a line on his operation."

"What good's knowing that Frank Hayward has Sutton allegiance? Everybody in this half-pint town has taken sides."

"I know," Tallman said as he exhaled a long stream of smoke. "But I still have that dead Ranger in mind. Somehow, it doesn't fit. Why bother to kill a Texas Ranger who is investigating a feud? It's no great secret as to who's on whose side. So what did the man know that caused someone to tie him to a tree and shoot him in the forehead? It's got to be more than the feud."

Vivian paused and became pensive. She'd never picked up on that angle. It didn't make any sense unless there was something they were overlooking.

"Someone like Nate Gill and his followers would love to see Trowbridge send troops into DeWitt County. It would be proof that the man is the scoundrel Gill says he is," Vivian said.

"The thought hasn't passed me by," Tallman added. "The idea's been stewing, but right now there sure as hell isn't a damn thing to hang my hat on. In any event, I suggest we give ourselves until Sunday night. If we have nothing by then, we'll can this operation and get on the trail of Mr. John Wesley Hardin. I know Pinkerton would approve. He doesn't cotton to losing two of his men." He took another sip of the whiskey. "So let's find out what we can about the feud. And let's take a special interest in Hardin. We'll start to dog him on Monday unless there is something to keep us here."

"That suits me," Vivian said. "I don't feel at ease in this preacher role."

"Speakin' of religion! You haven't mentioned our Mr. Garwood," Tallman asked. "What did you find out?"

"Baptist men are just as interested in a lady's private parts as any man," she teased.

"Baptist, Methodist, or nonbeliever. You cast a mighty powerful spell on a man," Tallman added with a sigh.

"You included?"

Tallman raised his dyed eyebrows and chuckled.

"Tell me what else you found out about Sheridan Garwood."

Vivian shrugged and proceeded to tell her fellow Pinkerton that she felt as if she'd learned nothing except that Garwood's outward appearance was nothing more than fresh-laid horse apples. "But all he'll say about the feud is that it's raising hell with business in town. I gather both the Suttons and the Taylors are behind on their payments to the bank."

"That can't be good from his point of view," Tallman injected.

"You might not think so. But I have found out that Garwood has his mind set on getting into the cattle business."

"Like every other dreamer in Texas."

"But Garwood has the edge on any dreamer. The way I understand it, Garwood is circling overhead waiting until the war has ruined its soldiers. Then he plans to swoop in and pick their bones clean."

Tallman smiled as he exhaled a cloud of cigar smoke. Vivian was a damned good agent.

"Of course he's not the only one. There's a runt of a Scotsman who's also waiting aloft on the thermals."

"Gill," Tallman grunted.

"He flat out told me he's taking great pleasure in watching the Taylors and the Suttons shoot it out. He claims that he'll be in the front row at the auction. Garwood seems to think that Gill has a load of money

Matt Braun

behind him too. Though he doesn't know where Gill gets his financing. Garwood claims that Gill won't even set foot on the plankwalk in front of the Cuero Safe Deposit, let alone step inside."

"Hmm," Tallman groaned as he pulled on the cigar wedged in his teeth. "There sure are a lot of people who might profit from the feud."

"Bankers to bullet makers. One man's loss is another man's gain."

The wolf takes down the prey, gets his fill, and the vultures swoop in for the pickins, Tallman thought to himself. He was beginning to wonder if Nate Gill might be the wolf *and* a vulture.

FOURTEEN

The horses chugged on effortlessly, seeming to enjoy the morning air. When Tallman reached the bridge just south of the fork where Sandies Creek came into the Guadalupe, he crossed as the stableboy had directed him to. He was to follow Sandies Creek for five miles and then turn in at the marker, a large copy of Taylor's "JT" brand burned into a board which was nailed to the gatepost.

But he hadn't gone a mile beyond the bridge when he got the distinct feeling that someone was dogging his path. As he drew a thin cigar from his vest, he thought that Taylor would have to be a fool not to have guarded the approach to his ranch. He scratched a sulfurhead on the carriage seat, lit his cigar, and proceeded boldly.

His suspicions were confirmed when two horsemen appeared from behind a clump of trees, ambled into the grassy hump between the twin ruts and stopped.

Tallman slowed the carriage and then pulled the horses to a halt only a few feet from the pair of riders.

"Howdy, boys!" Tallman said cheerfully, as if their blocking the road was an invitation for a friendly chat.

"Where you headed, mister?" the one in the silver-studded saddle asked.

"Well, now," Tallman said in his slightly overdone New York accent as he flicked the ash from his cheroot, "I'm not sure what my plans have to do with you gentlemen." He'd decided to shoot the talkative one first if it came to that.

"Did ya hear that, Lem?" the loud one asked his sidekick. Then he looked back at Tallman. "Looks like we got us some sort of foreigner here."

"Where you from, dude?" Lem asked from atop his plain saddle.

"New York," Tallman answered, trying to appear foolishly undaunted by the riders. "And I have business to attend to. So if you fellows will move your horses, I'll be on my way."

"Damn, Lem. Don't he sound some funny!"

"You ain't on your way, mister, until you tell us what you're up to," the one called Lem said in a monotone. "In case you ain't heard, we got a war on here in DeWitt County. There ain't no flags and uniforms, so it's some hard to tell the enemy."

"The Sutton-Taylor debacle!" Tallman exclaimed, his voice projecting delight. "I assume you gentlemen would be Taylor warriors then."

The two horsemen looked at each other with raised eyebrows and put-on grins. The one in the flashy saddle asked Lem: "What the hell's a de-bake-el?"

"It's what you people in DeWitt County are faced with," Tallman went on, ignoring the jab. "I'm here to see James Taylor. Research on my book on the feud. Now maybe you gents can help me?"

"We're with him," Lem explained. "Now just who the hell are you?"

"Henry Ravensdale. I make my living as a writer."

"You doin' a book on Jim?" the other sentry asked, his mood less sour.

"I'm recording all the events surrounding the feud and preparing sketches of all those involved. Now if you'll please lead the way. I don't have forever. The people back East are waiting to know more."

Both riders perked up at the thought of being written up in the history books. The one in the flashy saddle introduced himself as Mannin Clements and went on to introduce his partner as Lem Davis.

"Mr. Clements! I've heard of you! We must talk after I've had a talk with Jim Taylor and Bill Sutton,"

Tallman said. He appeared to ignore Davis, but he was, of course, pleased to have learned the identity of the Texas Ranger who was working undercover for the governor. He doubted that Davis had any idea that he was one of the two Pinkertons.

After another minute of chatter, the pair led Tallman down the road to the Taylor ranch house.

Taylor appeared on the porch when the famous Mannin Clements shouted their arrival. The sentry quickly explained who "the slicker from New York" was and jabbered on to Taylor about "bein' wrote up in books."

"Step down, Ravensdale," Jim said in a tired monotone. Then he looked at Davis. "Take care of his rig and his horses, Lem."

"Sure, boss," Davis answered.

Tallman followed Taylor into the house, especially content with his writer con. *Vanity*, he thought to himself, always works.

Taylor appeared worn out. Though he was still on the sunrise side of thirty, he looked older. His skin was well-weathered and deep creases swept away from his narrow eyes and went right into his long, curly, sun-bleached hair. He looked like he was squinting all the time. His other features were sharp and distinguished, especially his straight nose and jutting chin. It was the kind of face, though not pretty, which would give a woman cause to take a second look.

"Sit down, Ravensdale, and tell me what you want," Taylor commanded. Then, before Tallman could edge in a word, Taylor turned toward the kitchen and shouted: "Darlin'! Bring two glasses and a bottle."

Taylor had no sooner slumped into his chair when his plain-looking wife arrived with a neutral expression on her face. Tallman popped out of his chair like an eastern gentleman and introduced himself. "Henry Ravensdale, Mrs. Taylor. A pleasure to meet you." She smiled at the gesture.

"Have a seat, Florence. This here fellow is writin' a book on the feudin'."

Her face became a mask of cold resignation. Tallman guessed that he hadn't seen such sad eyes in a decade.

"Well . . . Ah . . . Mrs. Taylor, that *is* why I am here. I don't mean to upset you."

She looked at the writer, her face unchanged.

Tallman went into a quick explanation of his mission. "We're all so civilized back in Boston, Philadelphia and New York. We long for some of the excitement of the emerging West!"

"Ain't much to share," Taylor's wife muttered. "Us womenfolk just sit by and watch our men act like a

149

pack of damn-fool kids and wait for the day when Harry Edelbrock will box 'em up and we'll be throwed off the ranch."

"Goddamn it, Florence! Don't talk that way," Taylor groaned as he dragged his leathery fingers through his curly hair. "This here fight is more than *that!*"

Hoping to cool Taylor, Tallman took out a pad and asked the rancher to start from the beginning.

The man gladly complied. For over an hour, he explained his view of the origin of the feud and then the events of the summer. The tale didn't vary much from what Tallman had heard before.

"So it was calm up until Bill Sutton's brother-in-law, Jake Hawkins, was shot by the men who burned his barn?" Tallman asked.

"It had been over a year," Taylor agreed as he tossed back the rest of his whiskey.

"Your boys do that?"

"No way, Ravensdale," Taylor insisted.

"Who, then?" Tallman asked. "You sure as hell got blamed for it!" Oddly, Tallman sensed that Taylor was telling the truth.

"Don't rightly know, Ravensdale. And I don't rightly give a shit as long as the Suttons roast in hell."

Taylor's wife looked up from the sewing she'd been doing and gave her husband a look that would have scared off a rabid wolf.

"There's plenty of Taylors in these parts," Taylor

said, ignoring his wife's cutting gaze. "And even though Sheriff Pete Kelly is softer than fresh-dropped cow shit, I don't expect a man would be mouthin' off about who he killed. We still got us some lawdogs hereabouts that might try to do somethin' about it if a man were to brag about killin' Jake Hawkins."

"You did shoot Sutton in Bank's?" Tallman asked bluntly.

"Fair and square. He had about the same chance as my Daddy. Only sorry he ain't dead and gone to hell yet."

"Sure wish I had a line on who got Hawkins," Tallman said. "Maybe you could give me a clue or two? Who might I talk to in order to find out?"

"Likely my kin or one of my friends. But I surely don't know any more than that."

"Hawkins wasn't a Sutton though."

"His old lady, June, is Bill Sutton's little sister. That makes him a Sutton," Taylor grunted as he filled his glass and then topped up Tallman's drink.

"The thing that makes it interesting from my point of view as a storyteller is that it was the first incident in the recent outbreak of fighting," Tallman went on, hoping for more.

"Probably your cousin, Wes Hardin, or one or another of them no-accounts you always got hanging around here like bees on spring flowers," Taylor's wife spat, her mousy face drawn and her shrill voice ringing hollow with a sense of despair and defeat. "One of them that shot that dear Doc Blanchard and his wife and child! Those poor people."

"Goddamn it, Florence! Shut up!" Taylor interrupted his wife.

Tallman thought he was on the verge of wringing her slender neck.

She returned a nasty look and went back to mending the shirt in her lap.

"I was going to ask you about Doc Blanchard and his family. And now that your wife has brought it up—"

"That ain't my kind of doin'," Taylor broke in. "He was good friends with Sutton and someone must have thought that was reason enough to kill him. But I ain't never backshot no man and, for sure, no woman and fifteen-year-old kid!"

Tallman took out a cigar and lit it, slowly puffing the end to a glowing ash. Though he believed Jim Taylor, he couldn't help notice the satisfaction in Taylor's eyes each time he mentioned the demise of another Sutton friend or kin.

"Hell, mister," Taylor said when he saw the pensive look on Tallman's face. "This here feudin' has got bigger than any one of us. People have taken up sides. Even people who don't know me!"

Tallman listened to the explanation. But he didn't

accept the fact that some disinterested party would blow a man and his womenfolk from their carriage simply out of a sense of loyalty to a family they didn't even know. It didn't make sense.

Tallman continued to quiz the man for a while longer, all the time pumping him up with talk about how he was becoming part of history. When Taylor mentioned his father, his face was twisted into an evil mask and he swore fiendish oaths of retribution.

"I'm plannin' to cut that bastard's heart out and feed it to the pigs!" he growled after Tallman asked for more on the slow and painful death of Pitkin Taylor. "Pig shit is what he'll be!"

Taylor's wife got up and ran from the room, allowing her sewing to fall to the floor.

Seizing the opportunity, Tallman asked a personal question. "The whole thing appears to place a terrible strain on the family, Mr. Taylor," Tallman noted with the tone of a preacher about to counsel a fresh widow on the nature of God's will. "And it sure can't be good for the cattle business."

Taylor looked across at Tallman as if to suggest that the interview had just ended.

Tallman returned the gaze. "I'm just trying to get a feel for the rage you must experience, the problems you must face. I want the book to be more than an account of a few shoot-outs. I want people to *know* Jim Taylor."

"Well, then, mister," Taylor said as he got up, "you just hang around for another week or so and you'll have the endin' to your story as well as a good idea about who Jim Taylor is. I'll be puttin' a stop to this goddamned thing once and for all. Got to—so's my daddy can rest in peace."

Tallman stood, retrieved his black bowler, and extended his hand. Then he pushed hard. "Good luck to you, Mr. Taylor. And I hope I didn't offend you with that last question. It's just that I could see your wife doesn't seem to take much pleasure in the feudin' business, and—and, well, folks in town have been talking about the financial difficulties the Suttons *and* the Taylors are having. It's no fun to have the bankers nippin' at your backside."

"I ain't got no love for bankers in general. But then I ain't got no complaints about mine either. Sheridan Garwood has been good to us. Fact is, he's ridin' out the bad times with us." Taylor paused and rubbed his weathered chin. "Long as I don't have to hear none of his church bullshit!"

Tallman smiled, turned and went for the door. Just before he went through the opening, he stopped and turned to Taylor. "Oh," he said. "Just one more thing. I ran into a man in town earlier, Frank Hayward. And I forgot to ask him. Has he taken up sides?"

"Not that I know. Guess he does some work for

Nate Gill from time to time. Mostly he just hangs around lookin' clean and tidy. Don't guess he'd join in for fear of gettin' his pretty duds dirty."

Tallman tipped his bowler and left.

FIFTEEN

On the way back to town, Tallman puzzled over his meeting with Jim Taylor. It was obvious that just being near the feudists was akin to playing with a teased-up sidewinder. Taylor was hell-bent on destroying the Sutton family and anyone who had ever bade them a friendly hello. And if his family and all of DeWitt County went up in flames, Taylor was willing to pay the costs.

As the pair of gray horses pulled him into the south end of town in the snappy rig, he recalled the desperation in the face of Taylor's wife. She was planning for the worst.

Though it was only late afternoon, the south end of Cuero was coming alive early. It was Friday. The town was filling up with men who had a mind to spend a week's wages before the Saturday sunrise. On the right, lively music flowed from the faded yellow frame building which was marked boldly by a large black-on-white sign, announcing in gothic letters: MAYBELL'S DANCE HALL. And in smaller letters below it said: *Girls*.

"Hey, Slick," one of the scantily clothed women shouted from the balcony. "You wanna take a lady for a ride in that big-city rig of yours?" She was leaning so far out over the railing that her pancake breasts swung out of her loose, dark red gown.

Tallman cracked a toothy grin, tipped his bowler, and diverted his attention to Bank's. Though the trio of black musicians hadn't yet arrived, the din which filled the street suggested that the place was half full and that several of the heavy drinkers had been there for a while. Likewise, the Red Dog, separated from Bank's by an empty lot, was pouring the whiskey fast and furious.

As he went by the establishments, he chuckled to himself. Nobody ever went broke owning a saloon or a whorehouse. He was several buildings past Bank's when he remembered that he ought to have a look at the walls in the shithouse behind the saloon and billiards parlor. Davis had said that he and Mannin Clements were going to town that afternoon. He urged his handsome team into a U-turn in front of Nate Gill's real estate office. When he saw Gill's sign, he recalled what Jim Taylor had said about Hayward working for Gill from time to time.

As he hitched the team to the post in front of Bank's, his mouth began to water at the thought of a cool draught. When he stepped through the bullet-splintered batwings, the first thing he heard was Tinker Morton. The fat hulk was boasting on a bellyfull of cheap whiskey about how he was going to cut somebody's throat. Tallman suspected that the somebody was Turk Willis.

He ordered a draught. The saloon girl who'd spent the night in the loft with him was nowhere to be seen.

After quickly swallowing the cool ale, he made for the back door. The outhouse vapors hit him from ten paces out. Once inside and breathing carefully through his mouth, he scanned the marked-up walls wondering how he would ever find anything among the numerous carved obscenities and penciled insults which covered the fly-spotted boards. Down further, his eye caught fresh-cut words: *Texas Rangers shovel horseshit and howl at the midnight moon.*

Original, Tallman thought. The livery at midnight.

Before setting out, Tallman stopped by Vivian's room and explained that he was going to Hallstetter's Livery on the assumption that the Ranger would be there.

After Vivian stopped kidding him about his hanging around outhouses, he briefed her on his meeting with Taylor.

"I'm going on the assumption that there is more to this than a family feud," Tallman insisted. "It makes no sense any other way. The way Taylor's wife reacted to the killing of the Blanchard family caused me to reconsider. You don't blast a fifteen-year-old girl into kingdom come because her father is friendly with one of the feudists. That kind of killing means big money, big politics . . . big something."

"I get that feeling," Vivian agreed. "But I sure don't have any idea what the alternative might be."

Tallman went on to explain his theory about political skulduggery of some sort. When Jim Taylor had mentioned that Frank Hayward had worked for Nate Gill and that he had no loyalty to the feudists on either side, something had clicked. Hayward was burning barns for someone. Vivian listened carefully.

"I know you doubt that we'll find a reason for this killing and burning, Viv," Tallman said. "I'm convinced it's a long shot. But what the hell. We're on our way Monday morning if we have nothing by then. That is, unless you can convince your banker friend that it is in his best interest to set up a Monday meeting between Jim Taylor and Bill Sutton."

"Are you crazy?"

"Last time I pondered on it, I didn't think so," he said with his square white teeth beaming from under his paste-on mustache. "And I've only got ten minutes until midnight. So hear me out."

Vivian sighed. She had been hoping to pull Tallman into the goose down. The tension in her loins had been growing by the minute.

"Just listen carefully," he said, giving her a friendly scolding. "Here's the angle. It seems to me that the feudists are broke or damn near broke. There hasn't been much cattle business tended to this summer. And they must use Cuero Safe Deposit Company as their bank. I know Taylor does. So you are going to hustle your Mr. Garwood tomorrow and convince him that it is in the best interest of everyone to meet to discuss the financial difficulties. Tell him he'll never get to heaven unless he tries. Tell him anything that works."

"I don't know," she said softly, her voice trailing off.

"Hell, tell him to threaten the feudists with foreclosure. I have confidence in you, Viv. I've never seen a man who could resist you. And make sure you get to the meeting. I'll wedge my way in as the man who's going to record the great moment in history."

"Jesus, Ash," she groaned.

"Look, Viv," his tone becoming less tolerant, "we might stop this thing and be on our way by Tuesday or Wednesday. If we can't force a meeting, we still set out Monday morning. Thanks." Tallman got up, kissed her on the forehead and left the hotel room.

Once out on the street, he circled around behind the hotel. He wanted to approach the livery from the back. Cautiously, he made his way south in the distinct shadows of the buildings. The moon was high, nearly full, and encircled by a giant aura. The noises increased as he got closer. It was minutes before midnight and the sporting crowd was at full throttle. The music coming from the town's two saloons and single whorehouse merged in a strange rattle of sharp sounds.

Tallman undid his coat as he approached the livery. Stopping short of the row of wagons parked behind the barn, he pulled his .41 Colt from it's spring-loaded leather and checked the chambers. All were loaded with Wagner's explosive-tipped shells. As he clicked the cylinder back in place, Tallman thought of the fate of several of his previous victims when hit with the diabolical bullets. They made a certain mess.

Satisfied with the readiness of his Colt New Line, and reassured by the feel of the derringer on his right forearm, he holstered the gun and moved slowly forward, always seeking the cover of the moon's shadows. Once he had reached the back of the barn, he looked about and surmised that he was alone.

For five minutes he waited, leaning quietly against the rough-cut barn boards. The horses stirred, chomped on their hay, occasionally slopped in their water buckets, and snorted loudly. But there were no human sounds. Becoming discontented with the wait,

Tallman walked carefully into the moonlit area on the south side of the barn. The livery was the last building on the street and all that lay between him and the flat-lands to the south were two steaming manure piles. As he walked slowly past the first heap, he heard a footstep.

Instantly, he spun to his left, drew his Colt, and fell to one knee, all in a single fluid motion. Then he heard the sound of the spur again. Only this time it was accompanied by a gruesome moan. After a quick span of the area, he moved around the second pile of manure. That's when he saw a man flat on his back. Only his leg moved, a spurred boot heel slowly scratched at the hard earth as if the man was trying to walk away from death. A large knife had been driven into his chest . . . to the hilt.

Tallman rushed forward after another quick look around. When he knelt beside the man he saw it was Lem Davis. His eyes were glazed, short quick breaths made an odd whistling sound, and his face was twisted in an agonizing death mask.

"Davis," Tallman whispered loudly as he leaned forward. That's when he saw that the Ranger's throat had been slit from ear to ear. Though the killer had missed the arteries, Davis's windpipe had been laid open. Each short breath caused air to whistle past the oblong hole in the white cartilage as blood gurgled slowly into the hole.

"Who did it, Davis?" Tallman commanded. "I'm the Pinkerton on the case. *Davis!* Who did it?"

Davis tried to say something and his eyes moved toward Tallman.

"Sutton's men?"

Tallman thought he saw Davis issue a slight negative nod before the whistling and the moving leg stopped abruptly. The Ranger's eyes rolled back, and he died.

"Shit!" Tallman cursed as he looked around again. When he looked down again, he saw the knife. It was the one he'd taken from Tinker Morton and given to Hayward.

With a renewed urgency, he turned Davis's pockets, and finding nothing he disappeared back into the shadows of the town's buildings.

SIXTEEN

It's a shame the rain spoiled our outing," Garwood said as he urged his horses toward his home on the outskirts of Cuero.

Vivian didn't hear him. Her mind was still occupied by the news Tallman had brought her. With the second Ranger dead, the whole case had taken on a nasty stench. They both had decided that the governor was somehow involved, either directly or indirectly, and that the DeWitt County chaos was more than a simple family feud.

"Isabelle," Garwood sighed. "You look as if your mind is two counties away."

"Oh . . . yes . . . I know," she stumbled. "I was just thinking about that poor man they found this morning behind Hallstetter's Livery. It's as if Satan himself has a grip on the town. I heard people talking about the man during breakfast in the hotel. They sounded like onlookers at a chess game. They talked about him as if he were a mere wooden figure to be removed from the board." She looked carefully at Garwood for some sort of reaction. She saw nothing, nothing but the usual glint of energy which constantly amused her. His wavy, soft hair, his eyes and his suntanned skin made him look more like an adventurer than a banker.

"Play with fire and you'll get burned," he said after a pause.

"That's not a very Christian response," she said bluntly.

Horseshit, Garwood thought to himself.

But she saw the disdain in his eyes and on his ruddy features.

"It just seems that there's no stopping this brutality and it can't be doing anyone any good. You saw what the governor's early morning telegram said!"

"I didn't," Garwood replied quickly. He was suddenly very interested.

"It was in the morning *County Democrat*. He's considering asking General Sherman to move troops into DeWitt County. He said the killing of his Ranger was the last straw."

Garwood was suddenly pensive and distracted.

"It seems to me that that would be awful. It would seem like the Civil War again."

"Yes, it would," he sighed as he pulled up the

horses in front of the large home which sat among several oak trees. "Very bad."

"Maybe they'll at least stop the killing," Vivian said, looking for further reaction.

She still wasn't sure whether his heart was black enough to intervene in a way to promote continuing feuding. Tallman had given her an assignment and she wanted to do her best. She was determined to convince Garwood that a Sutton-Taylor meeting was a must.

"Take care of the horses, Chiquito," Garwood said to the Mexican boy who came running up through the puddles. "And then clean up the buggy."

"*Sí*," the lad responded.

Garwood helped her down and the pair quickly moved out of the rain to the cover of the porch. Once under the roof of the large veranda, she pushed back her blue bonnet and waited for Garwood to open the massive door which hung on large hammered brass hinges. The large single-floor home was made of carefully cut and fitted southern pine logs.

"Why, this is beautiful," she said honestly when they entered the wide-open living area. "So unusual for this part of the country."

"Georgia yellow pine," he said. "It'll be here forever. The owner was killed in the war. Full colonel in the Rebel Army."

"*Señor*," a pretty Mexican girl greeted him after

she came through a door at the back of the room. "Let me have your coat." Then the dark-haired woman saw Vivian. "Yours too, please," she added with a slight sneer.

Vivian suddenly knew what Garwood did to expend his sexual energy when he wasn't in pursuit of itinerant lady missionaries. At least, she thought, he has fine taste. The housekeeper had beautiful brown eyes, long, soft black hair, and features that suggested an Indian heritage. It was obvious that she felt something for Garwood.

"Teresa," Garwood said with a forceful note in his voice, "you may have the afternoon off if you wish."

"Yes, Mr. Garwood. Chiquito and I will go to town."

That settled quickly, the Baptist deacon went for the cut crystal decanter which was half full of amber fluid. "Brandy?" he asked as the house girl disappeared. "The best money can buy!"

She agreed to a small snifter.

Garwood sat down with his glass and had Vivian join him. Then he quizzed her on what she'd read in the morning *Democrat*. It surprised her. It was the first time since they'd met that he initiated any discussion about the feud. Vivian explained what she'd read, embellishing slightly as she went on, always leaning toward the financial disruption the conflict was causing. Then she tried again. "Sher, it seems to me that you have the ideal opportunity to become the hero in this whole thing. Why don't you use your influence to put a stop to it?"

"I've tried many times," he said in a monotone. "They aren't about to listen to me."

"You told me that June Hawkins, Horace and Jim Taylor, and Bill Sutton all have their mortgages with you."

"So?"

"So, it seems to me that you have a means of getting some agreement from them . . . an extension of time if the fighting were to stop, for example."

"Why, that would be unethical!"

"For the love of the Lord, Sher. The whole feud is unethical. What's proper about killing?"

Garwood looked at the lady preacher and began to wonder. These were critical times for him and his plans to own the biggest spread in DeWitt County. "Also, Isabelle, you know that it's gone too far. The Suttons and the Taylors will not stop until they're all dead or gone." In that he was right. "You're no fool. You must know by now that I don't give a rat's ass whether or not those crude people meet their maker this very minute. They are all a lot of vile sinners and a just God will give them their due and leave the fruits of the land to those who deserve it."

"Meaning you?" she asked bluntly, showing no outrage.

"Whoever."

She allowed a quiet to overcome the large, open room as she stared at the banker. She knew it would do little good for her to play the Christian do-gooder. She guessed he probably had her pegged as a rip-off artist anyhow. So with crafty tenacity, she began to work another angle. "The love of money," she sighed.

"God never denied the pursuit of wealth as long as we give him his proper place at the top of the pyramid," Garwood said as he hoisted his glass aloft and drained the last of the exquisite brandy. "Seek and ye shall find."

For the next half hour, she angled Garwood toward realizing that it still might be in his best interest to call the meeting anyhow. "What will the people of Cuero think when the banker buys the grasslands he formerly held the notes on? You know how people look at bankers, especially since the war."

Garwood nodded with raised eyebrows.

She saw that he was listening. Then she struck a chord which let her know she had her mark. "Nate Gill and others intend to get that land also."

"What?" Garwood said as he came out of his chair.

"He told me so at breakfast one morning. He invited me to his table when the dining room was full. Said he'd be at the auction with a sack of money. And surely there must be others smart enough to see the profits to be made from the misfortune of others."

Garwood filled his snifter halfway and took a large gulp. Then he began to pace the floor. After several minutes he stopped in front of her and looked down. "You know, Isabelle, I can think of a better way for you to make a living than selling Bibles." He held out his hands in a way that compelled her to take them. He pulled her firmly to her feet. "Nobody, not even Nate Gill, nobody's going to stop me. And I think you see that. There's much more to your mind than you let on. Much more than your Christian con game."

Vivian tensed up at the truth and Garwood felt her respond.

Overcome by her closeness and the aura of evil he'd detected by her tenseness, he leaned over and kissed her soft lips, his tongue probing frantically and deeply, while his hand squeezed her firm breast feverishly.

"Oh, Sherrrr. We shouldn't," Vivian groaned, her voice revealing her increasing desire. "Reaaally."

Garwood looked momentarily into her hazel eyes and then lifted a breast out of its cup. He held the firm orb and began to gently suck on her swollen nipple.

Vivian groaned and moved her hand to the back of his neck and gently pushed his head into her breast. "Ooooo, Gawwwd," she groaned. She was enjoying Garwood's hungry sucking, but she thought she ought to make at least one more protest.

"Sher!" she said as she backed away. "You promised! I told you it's as hard for me to resist as it is for you."

"Bullshit," Garwood grunted, his eyes fixed on hers. "You wouldn't have come out here with me if you didn't want it." His tone was not that of the Baptist deacon. His voice was punctuated with an animal urgency. The real Garwood had been laid bare. "You love a big stiff cock as much as any woman and don't deny it."

"Oh, Sher," she said, faking a mild dismay, "weakness of the flesh is something we must fight."

Garwood smiled like a riverboat gambler who's just bluffed his way into a large pot with a pair of deuces. He picked her up and carried her to his bedroom where he set her on the bed and roughly pulled her clothing from her supple body and threw it on an expensive chair. Once he had her nude, he stared down on her and saw the wetness in her womanhood. She faked an erotic look of resignation and covered her breasts gently with her long fingers.

Slowly, the banker dropped his clothing on the colorful Spanish rug and looked at his prey.

Vivian resisted showing her soaring urgency and nearly lunged at Garwood when the handsome chunk of man dropped his drawers and she saw his thick, blood-engorged cock, a large drop of his seed already glistening on the swollen tip.

Garwood leaned down toward the soft mattress

and firmly grasped her ankles. He pulled her around so that her legs dangled over the side of the bed when he dropped them. Then he knelt between her long legs and forced them wide apart.

"Ooh, Sherrrr. Oh, no! What are you going to do?"

Garwood spread the lips of her wet opening with his thumbs and buried his lips in her. Then he stabbed his tongue into the opening and sucked her dripping petals.

"Gawd, Sher," she moaned as she pushed her pelvis hard onto his darting tongue. "Ahh," she moaned, her voice trailing off. "I'm . . . delivering . . . my . . . self . . . to . . . the gawd . . . damned devil." Then she grunted like a woman possessed and began to push rhythmically at Garwood's sucking lips. Then she held his head with superhuman strength and locked his face into her spread-open cunt.

Garwood was carried to oblivion by her grunting over the devil. He sucked and probed feverishly anticipating the moment when her juices would gush forward as they had the day he'd mounted her next to the stream. He'd never had a woman who carried on as she did.

"Ooh, damn, suck me, Sher," she growled, then she began jolting and shuddering as waves of pleasure flowed from her body, each spasm pumping discharge from her. "Now, Sher," she grunted as she released his head and scooted back on the bed. "I want you now," she said urgently as she put her legs in the air and spread them as wide as they'd go.

Garwood knelt on the bed and moved forward until she could rest her calves on his broad shoulders. With his cock in his hand he slowly rubbed his tip from one end of her crack to the other. Then, at her opening, he thrust with all his energy, plunging the huge prick deep into her. Then he withdrew slowly. Almost out of her, he jammed her again. Then again. And again.

Vivian was on fire with lust. Ripples of pleasure began to grow into waves as Garwood plunged into her depths and fingered her nipples greedily.

Slowly they climbed toward the zenith, and then, at the top, he squirted his hot seed into her womb as she pounded against him into a final all-consuming spasm. Spent, they both fell off the other side.

SEVENTEEN

As Tallman sat mechanically eating breakfast in the Gulf dining room, his mood had grown more sour with each passing minute as the rain beat down on the unpaved streets. The image of Lem Davis with the large knife protruding from his chest and the frothy hole in his neck was still clear in his mind. Davis was a symbol of a breach of security in the governor's office. Tallman's continued success as an agent depended on the promises he extracted from those he worked for. The minute more than one man knew of his identity, he considered the contract broken. As he chewed each mouthful of breakfast, he pondered the possibility that he might cancel Trowbridge's contract . . . permanently. If anyone but Vivian had known who Henry Ravensdale really was, they'd be on their way back to Chicago.

After he finished, he dashed across the muddy

street toward Nate Gill's office. When he leaped up onto the plankwalk in front, he stopped and slapped the rain off his bowler and took several moments to collect himself. It was then that he decided that Trowbridge would pay somehow. Maybe not with his life but somehow.

The board-and-batten building was one of the neatest in the backwater town. The smooth-planed yellow pine board-and-batten siding was varnished with an oil stain which had preserved the original color of the wood. A pale green trim gave the place a tidy appearance. Ornate gold leaf lettering on the glass upper half of the front door announced: *Nathan Gill, Real Estate.*

Tallman walked through the door as if it was *his* office. A prim young woman asked if she could help.

"Name's Henry Ravensdale. I'd like to see Mr. Gill."

"Oh!" the young woman exclaimed. "The writer from New York?"

"That's right, Miss Spencer," he said, reading her name from the brass plate on her desk.

"I read one of your books once . . . I think."

"Why, that's nice," Tallman said pleasantly. He was beginning to wonder if there *was* a pulp writer named Henry Ravensdale. "Mr. Gill available?"

"Oh . . . yes . . . one minute." She got up and

walked briskly to an enclosed office in the back of the room.

Tallman looked around the office with a detective's eye. He had become certain that some form of political skulduggery was aggravating the feud. One wall was covered with surveyors' drawings and topographical maps, sale notices, and several tinplate photographs of barns and houses. The opposite side of the room was lined with wooden file drawers on the bottom and bookshelves on the top. Until that moment he had no idea of what to say to Gill.

"What can I do for you?" Gill said as he approached with an outstretched hand. "Miss Spencer says you're the writer that has everyone talkin'."

Vivian was right. He did look like everyone's image of a leprechaun. Tallman felt odd towering over the little red-faced Scotsman.

"As everyone in Cuero seems to know, Mr. Gill, I'm here to do a book on the Sutton-Taylor matter. It's a big story back East."

"So I hear."

"And I wonder if you'd be willing to give me your impressions and possibly map out the land holdings of the feudists?" Tallman asked as he drew a cheroot from his coat pocket. "Cigar, Mr. Gill?" He held one of the expensive smokes out for Gill.

"Thank you, but I have my own," Gill said as he

pulled out one of his large cigars. "And it will be simple enough to get my impressions. The Taylors and the Suttons are a pack of damn ignorant fools. And I'll be able to show you exactly where their acreage is. I intend to buy it all when they finally have killed each other off."

Tallman looked carefully into Gill's green eyes for a sign but he saw nothing unusual. Gill radiated ambition and an overwhelming air of cynicism.

"You must not be a popular man in this town, Mr. Gill. As best I can tell, many in the county have taken sides."

Gill smiled, a cynical grin. "Everybody needs to belong, Ravensdale."

"I see," Tallman said, liking Gill more with each passing minute.

The small Scotsman looked at his watch. "Would you like a nip of good Scotch whiskey, Ravensdale? It's one o'clock and Saturday to boot!"

Tallman nodded approval and then he followed the jovial real estate man into his back office.

Lubricated by a large glass of Scotch, Gill began telling Tallman his version of the famous feud. It was about the same as he'd heard from others except that Gill openly declared that the feudists were a "passel of jackasses," and that he intended to be "at the auction with a fistful of banknotes."

"I don't see how the property will be worth much if DeWitt County is upside down," Tallman injected.

"This feud will run its course, Mr. Ravensdale. The cattle business ain't gonna die 'cause of a few flint-headed feudists."

Adroitly, Tallman worked Gill around to personalities, asking for character sketches of Jim Taylor, Bill Sutton, Horace Taylor, the deceased Doc Blanchard, the Clements, Wes Hardin, and Jake Hawkins, the first to die early in the summer when the long-standing feud was rekindled.

Gill admitted to knowing several of the feudists. Though he made it clear that he preferred to keep his distance.

"How about the town's peacemaker, Sheridan Garwood? I haven't had any time to get over to the bank to see him."

"Ha!" the small, stocky man bellowed in a quick, sharp wind. "That pompous son-of-a-whore. He couldn't settle a dispute between two alley cats with a ten-gauge shotgun!"

Tallman raised his eyebrows in an expression of surprise. "How did he come to be known as the peacemaker?"

"I guess he took it on himself. Bankers are that way. Since they ain't got a thing to do but count money and boot the widows and orphans off their

farms, they are always lookin' for some way to appear
to be doin' good. Somethin' so that they won't look
like the scum they are."

"What's that?" Tallman asked after he swallowed a
gulp of the smooth whiskey.

"Doin' good! There's no one human trait that com-
plicates the world as much do-goodin', especially
when it's practiced by Christian quacks like Garwood!"

"I'd guess that you and Mr. Garwood don't see eye
to eye?" Tallman asked, a thin smile showing under
the fake black mustache. "Seems to me that Cuero
Safe Deposit is the only bank in DeWitt County and
that you'd have to get on with Garwood."

"Got my own source of money, Ravensdale. You'd
not catch me walkin' 'cross the street to spit on the
front door of Cuero Safe Deposit," Gill snapped, his
Scottish brogue thick enough to slice with a knife.

Tallman said nothing in reply, hoping that Gill
would go on. He had begun to get a feel for the un-
dercurrents in the nebulous investigation. But Gill
simply shut up and pulled on his oversized cigar.

"Thought he was deacon in the church?" Tallman
went on after the brief silence. "A respected man in
the community?" Tallman was trying his best to bait
Gill.

"Any sidewinder slithering 'cross the desert sand

is more a creature of God than Sheridan Garwood. Lives north of town with a sharp-looking Mexican girl and her younger brother. Says she's the house-keeper, but everyone knows he's fuckin' her brains out. And you ought to see him sniffin' under the skirts of a female Bible merchant who arrived last week. I'd bet five double eagles that he's already had her britches off. In fact, I saw them ride out of town ear-lier. Probably hard at 'er right this very minute."

Tallman chuckled. Knowing Vivian, the ruddy lit-tle Scot probably wasn't far off the mark.

"How about Frank Hayward?" Tallman asked, sounding as if Hayward was nothing more than the next name on the list.

Gill looked at Tallman with an odd glance. Then he finished the warm Scotch in his glass.

Tallman's first reaction was that he'd caught him off guard.

"Who gave you Hayward's name?"

"Don't recall, Mr. Gill. It's just one of the many I've got on my list."

"As far as I know, Hayward hasn't taken sides. Looks to me like he just hangs around looking like a dry goods store dummy."

"What's he do for work?" Tallman asked, remem-bering what Jim Taylor had told him.

"Don't know that much about the man, Ravensdale! And I sure can't see how he might fit into your story," Gill muttered as the prim Miss Spencer walked in through the open door.

"Mr. Detwiler is here to see you," she said to Gill.

Without another word, Gill stood up, held out his little hand and said: "Nice talkin' to you, Ravensdale. Good luck on the book. Glad to see that folks are makin' a few dollars here and there on these milksop feudists. Does my heart good!"

Tallman left the office and stood for a moment on the wet plankwalk. Thunder rumbled overhead, punctuated by cracks of lightning, and the rain streamed out of the sky in gray sheets. He paused there to wait out the worst of the downpour before making his way to Hallstetter's Livery. Though he was sure there was something sinister about Gill, he had nothing specific except that he hadn't mentioned the fact that Hayward had done odd jobs for him in the past. But there was something about his reaction when he mentioned the name that left him uneasy.

EIGHTEEN

Three riders in rain slickers escorted Tallman from the gate to Sutton's sprawling ranch house.

An elderly Mexican maid met him at the door just as one of the riders led his horses and mud-splattered rig to the lengthy single-story barn.

The furnishings were in sharp contrast to the crudely appointed décor of Jim Taylor's home. The furniture was of a heavy oak Spanish design with brown leather upholstery. The floors were covered with colorful woven wool rugs. A huge fireplace covered a part of one wall at the end of the spacious living area. Tallman was especially taken with Sutton's gun collection. He recognized several of the pieces and knew that the man had a big investment hanging on the wall.

"Howdy, Mr. Ravensdale," Sutton said from his

laid-out position on the couch. He was partly covered by a light gray blanket.

Tallman nodded a hello and complimented the rancher on his guns. "Fine assortment of guns you have there, Mr. Sutton."

"That's a fact, mister," Sutton agreed. His voice was weak and raspy but his spirits seemed high. "'Course I ain't done much collectin' since Taylor put three slugs in me without no warnin'."

"He claims that he was giving you the same break you gave his father," Tallman said calmly. "Of course, I don't know any more than people tell me."

"Why, that little shit," Sutton growled. Forgetting his wounds, he bolted upright and swung his feet to the floor, wincing as he moved. "That goddamn runt!"

"Mr. Ravensdale. You'll have to leave if this interview is going to upset my husband," Elizabeth Sutton said sharply. She was a pretty woman, at least twenty years younger than Sutton, who was close to fifty-five.

"Goddamn it, Lizzie! I'm all right. Christ, I was out and around in the wagon yesterday. It ain't Ravensdale's fault that I can't wait to piss on Jim Taylor's grave!"

"Didn't mean to cause an upset, Mrs. Sutton," Tallman apologized.

"Ain't nothin' you've done, mister. It's just that I

lose my mind when I hear myself accused of back-shootin' Pitkin Taylor. I ain't never backshot a man in my life and I ain't 'bout to start now!"

"Are you saying you didn't ambush Mr. Taylor?" Tallman asked as he opened his notebook and put his pencil at ready.

"Hell, no!" the man grunted. "I wouldn't lure a man away from Sunday dinner with a cowbell just to shoot him in the back!"

Tallman believed the round-faced man just as he had believed Jim Taylor.

"Damn," Tallman sighed as if frustrated by Sutton's denial. "I'm having a hell of a time sorting this thing out for my book. Taylor openly admits to a number of the incidents between the two families. Yet he denies others just as you deny the incident in which Pitkin Taylor was killed."

"Like what?" Sutton grunted as he stood up and began to walk slowly back and forth.

"Bill, you shouldn't be up," his wife said, her voice firm and pleasant.

Sutton waved her off.

"For example," Tallman began, flipping over a page on his notebook, "he claims that neither he nor his men gunned down your brother-in-law, Jake Hawkins."

"Lying bellycrawler! He sure as hell made my little sister a widow."

Matt Braun

"Now, Bill," his wife said in a soothing and mellow voice. "Don't go gettin' yourself all worked up." Then she turned to Tallman. "Mr. Ravensdale. Please. I insist. Maybe you could come back tomorrow."

"Elizabeth!" Sutton said, color coming to his face for the first time. "This is my house and I'll not have you talkin' to a guest that way."

Tallman looked back toward Sutton, pulled a thin cigar from his pocket, and fired up the tip with a wooden match.

"What else did he deny?" Sutton asked after he had stared his wife into submission.

Tallman went on with the tale as he'd heard it from the young Taylor. Sutton injected an odd complaint but most of the time he listened carefully. After he'd got Sutton going, the rancher was anxious to tell his side of the story, especially the tales about the beginning of the feud years ago. But as he went on, it was obvious to Tallman that Sutton was tired of the whole thing. It was true that he hated Jim Taylor for the ambush in Bank's, but it was also clear that he didn't want to see the county go up in flames. He had enough years under his belt to be more reasonable about the whole thing than the younger Taylor.

When Sutton's story trailed off, Tallman asked for character sketches of the feudists, especially the gunmen aligned with his family.

186

"Hayward?" he asked after Sutton had finished praising Dirk Avery, his foreman and one of his most reliable guns.

"Who?"

"Frank Hayward. Can't remember how I got the name but I have him listed as one of your men."

"Not my kind of people," Sutton said in a matter-of-fact voice. "Does odd jobs. He does some two-bit legwork for Nate Gill every now and then."

"What do you think of the prospects of settling this thing without further bloodshed?" Tallman asked as he put his notebook away. He knew it was time to leave and he was just as glad to go since he wanted to talk with Sutton's younger sister before dark. "I mean, if you don't mind an outsider saying so, the whole thing seems like a waste of lives. A war where everyone loses."

"That's the smartest thing I've heard in some time, Mr. Ravensdale," Lizzie Sutton said.

Sutton grunted.

"Why can't you men smoke the peace pipe?" Tallman asked. "I interviewed the banker, Garwood, and he says he's been trying to act as peacemaker."

"That blowhard," Sutton said. "Him and his Praise the Lord bullshit!"

"Bill," his wife said. "That's not proper."

"Why that son of a bitch drinks as much whiskey

as the next man and he's fuckin' the britches off his Mex maid."

"William Sutton!" his wife said. "If it wasn't for Sheridan Garwood we'd be foreclosed on by now!"

NINETEEN

The road north to the Hawkins's JJ Ranch had turned into two small streams. Lightning streaked through the distant sky and the thunder sounded like random cannon fire. The matched grays kicked up mud and splashed water with every step. Though it was still two hours to sunset, the sky was dark.

Bill Sutton had deeded the land to his younger sister, June, when she'd married Jake Hawkins. It was the third largest cattle operation in DeWitt County. Though June had handled the management of the ranch since her husband was killed during an attempted barn burning early in the summer, rumor had it that she was in the worst financial straits of all the feudists.

When he pulled up in front of the house, an elderly man in a rain slicker approached from the direction of the bunkhouse with a Winchester cradled in his arms.

"Hep ya, mister?" he asked in a rickety voice.

"I'd like to see Mrs. Hawkins," Tallman said with a pleasant voice.

"She expecting ya?"

"No. She isn't sir. My name's Henry Ravensdale."

"The writer from Boston?" the man grumbled.

"New York."

The old man grunted and walked up to the door. After a brief conversation with the maid, he waited. Moments later the maid returned and said something to the man with the Winchester.

"Go on in, Mr. Ravendole," the man said, his voice tired and shaky. "I'll take your rig into the barn and hang a hay net for your horses."

The maid let him in and took his wet hat. Tallman was surprised when he saw the inside. It was an uncommon sight in Texas. The whole house was done in early colonial furniture. Hand-carved English walnut and elaborate upholstery was everywhere. He could have just as easily stepped into a pre-Revolutionary Virginia plantation.

"I'm June Hawkins," the woman said as she walked forward with her hand extended.

"Henry Ravensdale," he lied, fixing his gaze on her dark brown eyes, and accepting her firm handshake.

She was one of those women who would make any man sit up and take note.

"My pleasure," she said, her voice deeper than that of most women. "Please sit down. Brandy?"

"That might take the chill off my bones," he said. "I've been fighting Texas rain all day." He watched as she walked to an ornate walnut cabinet which stood on hand-carved eagle claws. Her long legs rose to a firm jutting hind end and every inch of her showed through the faded, tight-fitting stovepipe Levi's which were tucked into her cowhide boots. Long black hair fell over her red-check gingham shirt, stopping at her wide hand-tooled leather belt. She didn't look like a woman in trouble.

As she approached with the brandy, he admired her silver belt buckle and the matching bola which held a white apache tie close to her throat.

"I'm surprised to see such furniture in Texas, Mrs. Hawkins," Tallman said as he accepted the liquor. "It's beautiful."

"Please call me June," she said boldly as she sat in one of the wingback chairs. "And you are right, this gaudy stuff is rare. And I hate it!"

"I take it that your husband was the one who fancied the style then?"

"You are correct," she said bluntly.

Tallman couldn't help fixing his eyes on hers. "Brandy's excellent. You have good taste, and—"

"My husband again. I wouldn't know the difference," she said without a change in her expression. "He was the son of a South Carolina aristocrat. In fact the furniture is what was left of their possessions after the North rolled through. He didn't like the furniture either, but he felt some obligation to try to maintain the pieces. The caretaker of the family heirlooms or something like that."

"I see," Tallman answered.

"Now what can I do for you?" she asked as she crossed her legs.

Tallman went into his tale about the book, altering it slightly for her. He doubted he could appeal to her vanity. She looked like the sort of woman who had that under control. As he explained what he wanted, her spirits obviously sagged.

"To be honest with you, Ravensdale, I am so sick of this child's play that I doubt that I can offer you much. Jim Taylor, his old man, his uncle Horace, Wes Hardin, one of the Clements or some other ignorant son of a bitch shot the best man I ever knew . . . and for no good goddamned reason," she responded in a monotone.

Tallman sensed the mix of despair and venomous hatred. It was in her eyes.

"I'm sorry, June."

She nodded after taking a large swallow of the amber fluid in her glass.

After an ample portion of brandy, June Hawkins began to reveal her true feelings about the state of the fight and the effect it was having on her life. Angry resignation might best have described it. She explained that her men were driving five hundred head of longhorns northwest to the stockyards in Abilene on the rumor that East Coast buyers were planning large purchases that fall. She hoped that it would provide enough cash to get her through the winter.

It was obvious to Tallman that she enjoyed her new role as cattle rancher and he suspected that she'd do as well as any man, given a chance.

She set a small fire in the large stone fireplace "to take the chill and dampness out of the air."

Tallman watched as she crouched in front of the rugged stonework. He didn't need the fire. His body had been producing its own heat as he contemplated the idea of spending the night.

She had just put a match to the paper when two gunshots thumped in the damp air.

"Stay here," he said as he reached instinctively for his .41 Colt and lunged out of the chair. He ran out of the front door into the rain and immediately saw a lump on the ground in front of the bunkhouse. Advancing slowly, he surveyed the open ground, realizing that he had no cover.

It was the bunkhouse cook who'd called him Ravendole earlier that evening. His cap-and-ball

Remington still in his hand, he lay dead in the mud, his open eyes unflinching in the falling rain. A large red spot on his breastbone was awash in the heavy drizzle.

Then he heard a horse whinny frantically. He looked up and saw a glow in the dank air. Then smoke.

He ran for the blind side of the barn and turned the corner to face Frank Hayward who was holding a keg of coal oil. A small fire at the far end of the barn backlit Hayward. Both men froze. Then Hayward went for his gun as he dropped the keg. But Tallman fired twice before Hayward could get the Smith & Wesson American out of its fancy leather. The explosive slugs sent him spinning into the mud. As Tallman walked toward the groaning heap, an explosion at his back caused his heart to stop. Instinctively he spun on his heel and fell to one knee, just in time to see a man go face first, spread-eagle into the barnyard slop. June Hawkins stood calmly with a smoking twelve-gauge scattergun.

"You were about to go to heaven, Ravensdale," she said. Her face was cold and void of emotion.

"I can see that," he said, looking at the corpse. The man's back was smoking, ground meat.

Methodically, June Hawkins walked past Tallman and aimed the shotgun at Hayward's face.

"Jesus! Wait," Tallman commanded. Then he

bolted forward and rolled Hayward on his back, cocked the Colt and put it against Hayward's forehead. "Remember me, Frank?" Tallman growled.

"Willis," he grunted as blood seeped from the corner of his mouth. "You son of a b—"

"Who are you working for?" Tallman shouted in Hayward's face.

"Willis, fu—"

"It isn't Willis. Name's Ash Tallman. Now who are—"

"Fuck you," Hayward gurgled before he died.

Tallman's shoulders sagged and then he holstered his short-barrel Colt and looked at Hayward's dead face. "Shit," he grunted.

"The fire," she said suddenly. "Jesus! The fire!"

They both ran for the far corner of the barn and began slopping mud and water on the wall in what seemed to be a hopeless cause. Then the rain suddenly became so intense that they could barely see each other from five feet. The fire was suddenly extinguished as quick as a lamp run dry of kerosene.

Both stood looking dumbfounded.

A flash of lightning illuminated their sodden features and June Hawkins's face reflected her concern. "You have some explaining to do, Ravensdale or Willis or whatever the hell your name is."

"Name's Ash Tallman. I'm with the Pinkerton Detective Agency. We're in the hire of the governor of

Texas. I'll explain later but right now I think you ought to send out for the sheriff."

"I don't know what Pete Kelly can do," she said as they walked toward the two corpses. "He's worthless as squirrel shit," June exclaimed.

"Let's make it official nevertheless," he commanded.

The drenched woman looked at Tallman, sighed, picked up her shotgun where she'd dropped it and walked toward the house, slopping through the mud. "I'll send Juanita, my housekeeper. She's the only one left now that Pop's dead." Tallman heard her sobbing. "He's been with us since I was twelve years old."

Tallman went to the shotgunned body and turned the man's pockets. He found only a leather pouch containing several coins. Then he searched Hayward's pockets. Hayward's billfold was soaked so Tallman put it in his vest pocket and went for the cover of the barn. He wanted light to examine the contents of the thick leather wallet, and he had to ready his carriage for the maid.

Once through the large barn door, he found the lantern in a flash of lightning. He struck a match and fired the wick, filling the front of the barn with a warm yellow light. Under the flickering lantern, he carefully examined the contents of Hayward's billfold. It contained several banknotes and a thick, folded brown envelope. He undid the three folds and looked inside.

He saw fifteen one-hundred-dollar banknotes and a small wet note on plain paper: *Good work. But step up activity. G.*

"Nate Gill," Tallman said quietly.

TWENTY

Sheriff Pete Kelly had a blank expression as he loaded the three soggy bodies into the bed of his freight wagon. He could have been loading grain sacks.

June Hawkins explained exactly what had happened, leaving out the part about Tallman's admission that he was a Pinkerton agent. Kelly grunted from time to time. But he seemed distant.

"Both of you stop by the office early next week to sign papers," he said as he stepped up into the wagon. "Git up," he shouted at the team as he slapped the reins on their rumps.

"I see what you mean about Kelly," Tallman said to June as the wagon trundled off, its wheels cutting two thin grooves in the mud. Lightning went to ground nearby, causing a sharp crack and chest-thumping thunder. It was as if Mother Nature had decided to add an exclamation mark to Tallman's comment.

"Let's get inside before we're washed into the Gulf of Mexico," June said, water streaming off the back of her white Montana-peak Stetson. "You've got more explaining to do, Mr. Pinkerton man!"

As he followed, he couldn't help notice the movement under the soaked Levi's.

"I want to check on the kids," she explained as soon as she walked in the door. "Drop a couple of logs on the fire."

While she was in the bedroom with her two sons, Tallman again looked at the folded envelope and its contents. He was satisfied with his theory. Nate Gill had paid Hayward to stir up trouble among the feudists. Though he still couldn't picture Hayward murdering Doc Blanchard and his family or ripping open Lem Davis's throat, he'd surmised that it had to be. The fifteen hundred dollars appeared to be a single payment, likely one of many. That was annual wages for most.

When he heard her footsteps on the wooden floor, he stowed the envelope. He wasn't about to reveal *that* to anyone but Vivian.

"You were about to explain your theory when that lard-ass Kelly arrived," she said as she grabbed the brandy bottle. "I want to know what you're getting me into." She was barefooted and in dry clothing.

"I appreciate your confidence," Tallman said. "My progress would be halted if my cover were blown at this point."

Suddenly, she looked him up and down and began laughing. He suspected the brandy was having its effect. "For God's sake! You're soaked clean clear through!"

"Sure feels like it!"

She left the room and returned in a minute with a soft quilt. "Get your things off and hang them in front of the fire," she ordered as she handed him the colorful quilt. Then she dragged a chair forward and slapped her hand on the wingback: "Here!"

Tallman paused and then raised his eyebrows. "Mrs. Hawkins! We've just met!"

"I doubt you've got anything I ain't seen before," the tall and slender woman said as she turned away. "Give me the rest of your story while you're skinnin' out of your britches."

Tallman explained that he was sure that a third party had created many of the incidents which had caused the renewed hostilities between the families. He claimed that politics and land-grabbing were behind it.

"My problem is simple," he said as he flung the quilt around himself. "All the theories in the world aren't worth a bucket of horse apples in a courthouse. I need something to go on. Firm evidence."

"Do you know anything about who killed Jake?" she asked, her back to him. "These people—did they kill Jake?"

"I don't know for sure."

She spun and faced him. "Tell me!" Her eyes were flashing with anger.

"My guess is yes."

"Who?"

"Best I can figure, it was the man I shot tonight."

"But others are behind it?" she demanded.

Tallman swore that he didn't know and then pleaded for her help. He explained that he and his partner were trying to set up a meeting for Monday afternoon. He told her that his plan would only work if Bill Sutton and Jim Taylor were there under a temporary truce. "Now the way I see it, the hardest part of this whole plan will be to get that hot-blooded pair together. You can help. You've got to convince your older brother that he and Taylor are being used in a carpetbagger land-grab scheme. It's my only hope. Tell them that I have uncovered proof. That is, *Ravensdale* has the proof, not Tallman."

The fine-featured woman listened with a blank face. Then, as if someone had opened a valve, tears streamed from her eyes, her shoulders began bucking, and stifled sobbing pierced the quiet room. "Pop Mead used to tell me stories when I was a little girl," she sobbed, trying to compose herself. "What kind of an animal would gun down that nice old man?"

Tallman was usually uneasy around crying women, but in this case he understood. He stepped toward her and held her in his arms. "Hardly any profit in wondering on the nature of the beast. It's been the way of the world since Cain and Abel," he said.

Then she bolted away from Tallman. "You want my help, Ashley Tallman? You got it." Her eyes went dry and the color came back into her cheeks. "And forgive me for the tears. I know better than most that there's not a cent of profit in frettin' over spilt milk and gettin' carried off on memories." She walked to the wall and turned off two of the oil lamps and lowered the wick on the third.

"Life is here and now, this very minute," she said, her voice mellow again.

Tallman guessed that she'd spent many an hour pondering the tilt of the earth since her man had been murdered. And he'd decided that he would have liked Jake Hawkins. He had to have been a piece of work to get on with Bill Sutton's little sister.

Without warning she began to unbutton the clean blue and white gingham shirt she'd just changed into minutes earlier.

She began to feel a warmth in her loins as the detective's eyes fell to her hard little breasts. The large, dark brown nipples were erect. She felt their tension. It always amused her the way men seemed taken aback by the little mounds.

"You sure?" Tallman asked. "You've been riding the whirlwind for the past five hours."

She smiled and unhooked her hand-tooled silver belt buckle, lowered her clean Levi's, and stepped out of the heap. "I'm tired of having to do it myself," she said, thinking of the lonely nights she'd spent with only her slender fingers. "Damn it, I want a man in me!"

Quickly she pushed back the chair draped with Tallman's wet clothes. Then she pulled the cushions out of several others and threw them on the wool rug in front of the fire.

Tallman's eyes were fixed on her milk-white ass as she hurried about and then flung aside her shirt. Sleek as a young bobcat, she lay down in front of the fire and beckoned him with a naughty look and her wagging index finger.

She shuddered when the Pinkerton took one of her long nipples in his mouth and gently stabbed the brown bud with his warm tongue. The heat of the fire warmed her loins as she brought her feet up and spread her legs. When he put his hand on her silky black curls she pressed gently into his touch.

"Ooh, it's been so long," she said as she reached into his shorts for his stiff cock. She moaned when she felt the hot shaft and began to finger the wet tip. For her there was no experience to rival holding a man's swollen meat while sucking him to a feverish release.

Gently, she pushed his head away from her tiny breast. "I like to taste my man," she said as she shifted. "Just lay still."

While stroking him gently, she took the head of his cock between her lips and sucked, her tongue circling the end. The salty taste and the feel of the large knob in her mouth drove her wild. And when Tallman's hand found her damp curls again, she began losing control. Her strokes and her sucking became more vigorous and when he began to thrust upward into her greedy mouth, she felt surges of pleasure in her.

She groaned as if she'd just submitted to a horrible torture. Her hand pumped feverishly and she consumed his hot seed while she shuddered under his expert touch.

She was determined to make up for lost time.

TWENTY-ONE

A warm, gentle breeze ruffled the faded curtains in Tallman's room in the Gulf Hotel.

A noise on the street below jolted him upright in bed. He felt lost for a moment, unsure what day it was. Growing angry at himself for drinking beyond his limits and sleeping late, he stumbled to the plain pine dresser to get a look at his pocket watch. "Shit!" he grunted when he saw that it was a quarter past noon. He turned the tap on the tub and felt the water. Luckily the clerk hadn't fired up his steam pump and filled the tank on the third floor with cold groundwater.

By the time he made it to the crowded Gulf dining room, he was feeling better.

He ordered eggs and steak smothered in chili sauce and settled into his chair with a cup of fresh coffee. He hadn't been there five minutes when Vivian arrived with the Christian banker in tow.

Vivian had on her preacher outfit again—dark blue bonnet with matching straight skirt and heavily starched white blouse.

Only once during the meal did Vivian look his way. His train of thought, though, was interrupted several times by people who had some piece of "hard news" or a tall tale relevant to the famous feud.

Just as Vivian got up and went for the stairs, a woman stopped at his small table and began to spell her name: "B-L-A-S-S-E-R. That's Millie Blasser," she went on. "My daughter is married to a second cousin of Wes Hardin. And Hardin's kin to Jimmy Taylor. One of 'em what shot Bill Sutton!"

Tallman looked up with the expression of an addled stable hand and said: "Thanks Millie, I'll make a note of it."

"B-L-A-S-S . . ." she started again as he thunked a silver dollar on the table and left, pleased to leave a seventy-cent tip as long as he was able to escape most of the second spelling of the woman's name.

At the top of the stairs, he looked around and ducked into Vivian's room.

"Told Sher I had to powder my nose," she said as he came in.

"Sher is it?"

"Well," Vivian said with a sweep of her hand, "I'd guess we're on a first-name basis. He's all but proposed. Says he'll take me off the Bible circuit and make me queen of DeWitt County."

"That so?"

"Says we'll be worth a fortune by the end of the decade." Then she paused and her shoulders sagged. "But I guess I wasn't cut out to be the queen of the longhorns."

"I guess you're right," he agreed as he sat down and jammed an expensive cheroot into his teeth.

"Has he agreed to the meeting?" Tallman asked after lighting the thin cigar.

"No, sorry to say. And he seems terribly upset about something this morning. I haven't pushed too hard." Her eyes sparkled when she talked. "But he'll be working on it by sunset."

"Did you hear about what happened at the Hawkins ranch last night?" Tallman asked, assuming she had.

"No."

"Hayward and some two-bit gun tried to burn the barn."

"Hayward? What happened?"

"Dust to dust," Tallman said through a stream of smoke.

"The hired gun?"

"The Hawkins woman blew him near in half without flinching. She handles a scattergun with some authority."

He took the damp envelope from his vest pocket and held it out to Vivian. "Take a look. I found it on Hayward."

Vivian took the envelope and opened it. Her eyes widened when she saw the money.

"Read the note."

She unfolded the ink-smeared paper, read it quickly, and looked up.

"Nate Gill," Tallman said with a matter-of-fact timbre in his voice.

Vivian looked down at the paper again and her face became pensive. "Why not Garwood?"

"Doubt it, Viv. Gill's the one who's scrapping for real estate."

"Garwood seems pretty sure that he's going to be king of the cows someday."

"Doesn't everyone in this part of Texas?"

Vivian nodded and put the note back in the envelope. She didn't have Garwood pegged as a killer.

"I've got to get back," she said as she handed Tallman the envelope. "Sher has another of his riverside picnics planned for this afternoon."

"Be careful, Viv. We're playing with fire."

Vivian looked into his eyes and saw genuine concern.

"Things will really heat up when the *Democrat* hits the street tomorrow morning. I plan to leave a little something under the publisher's door this afternoon."

She took her purse from the chair and left without a word.

Tallman waited for five minutes before peeking out the door. Assured that the hallway was clear, he darted to his room. He wanted to write his note while the idea was still fresh in his mind. Standing at the dresser, he penned a short note on a piece of paper from his notepad:

Texas Ranger Lem Davis was on to carpetbagger land-grab plot when killed. Third party aggravating feud with random attacks on both Suttons and Taylors, hoping for the demise of all. Proof by Monday night!

After reading it over again, he folded the paper and put it in his coat pocket.

TWENTY-TWO

Vivian found great amusement in the lead story in the Monday morning *DeWitt County Democrat*. The headlines proclaimed in bold print: CARPET-BAGGER LAND GRAB? She knew immediately that it was Tallman's doing. If there ever was an idea that would put the whole town on edge, that was it. Everyone within earshot was jabbering on about the possibility, and that meant just about everybody in the Gulf dining room.

As she sipped her coffee she wondered again about Garwood. She'd convinced him to call a meeting by planting the idea that he'd look bad if he simply repossessed the ranches of the feudists without trying to resolve the problem. Frustrated by her refusal to allow him the pleasures of her womanly charms, and sure that Bill Sutton and Jim Taylor would refuse, he'd consented and sent a rider to each of the ranches late in the afternoon. Vivian hadn't seen Tallman since their brief meeting the day before when he'd shown her the fifteen hundred dollars and the note, and that had been playing on her mind.

Whatever he had done, she mused after finishing her poached egg on toast, it had been effective. Within three hours, the rider had returned from Bill Sutton's spread.

Sutton had agreed to meet. He had even sent a message to Jim Taylor, though it nearly killed him to put the pen to the paper. He said that it was carved in stone that they would hate each other forever. But both families had been loyal to the South. And that was enough to give them cause to stop to think when they'd heard about the possibility of a Yankee scalawag using their feud to rob them of their land. Tallman had counted on that.

Vivian paid her breakfast bill. Several people were waiting and she was anxious to get back to her room. She was sick of the lady preacher role. People either laughed at her or treated her to syrupy harangues about their Christian virtue.

She kicked off her shoes when she got to her room and then flopped on the bed. The Sutton-Taylor case had been a letdown after the rapid-fire action of her first two jobs with Tallman. She was contemplating her boredom when she heard a light tapping on her door.

"Who is it?" she asked as she padded to the door.

"Me," Tallman said bluntly.

Vivian let him in.

"I understand Garwood called the meeting. Nice work," he said.

"He sure seemed surprised when Sutton said yes."

"No doubt."

"Though he still thinks the meeting has been called to approach them about their financial difficulties."

"Hope it stays that way until two."

"See the paper?" she asked him.

"No."

"Have a look when you get a chance. The editor went wild. What on earth did you do?"

"Slipped a little note under the door," Tallman said.

"It should be some meeting," she sighed.

Bill Sutton came into town from the north. Though his mending wounds ached with the jostling he was getting atop his freight wagon, he held his head up proudly. At least twenty-five riders followed, dispersing along the length of DeWitt Street as they came through. The people of Cuero lined the main street to have a look at Sutton. The last time many had seen him was two weeks earlier when he had been hauled from Bank's in a bloody blanket.

Sutton tipped his hat to Garwood who was waiting

on the plankwalk in front of the Gulf Hotel. The big man winced as he stepped down from the wagon. "Stay here," he told the ranch hand still sitting up on the wagon bench. Then he turned to Garwood. "Let's get to it, Garwood," Sutton grumbled.

"I want to hear about these goddamned carpetbaggers in Austin." "What?" the banker asked, taken aback by the mention of carpetbaggers. He hadn't seen the *Democrat*.

Sutton gave Garwood a hard look and walked into the dining room without another word. Gill had had the hotel employees put several tables together and cover them with their best linen. The day before, Tallman had told the short red-faced Scot that Garwood was having a meeting to warn the feudists that their mounting debts could not be overlooked any longer. "If you're interested in that land, Mr. Gill, I'd make sure I was there to hear what the Baptist deacon has to say. Word has it he's out to grab the land for himself. They're using your hotel. You might as well look in."

He knew he had Cuero's vice-financier and real estate magnate hooked when his face went from its usual red glow to a deep purple.

A mile south of town, Jim Taylor pulled up his stock paint and held up his hand. His men stopped behind him. He took out Sutton's note and read it again:

The writer, Ravensdale, claims to have proof that carpetbaggers have been behind a lot of the killing and burning, including the ambush of your old man, and the murder of Jake Hawkins and the Blanchards. I want a truce for one day so we can hear him out. Tomorrow. Two o'clock, Gulf Hotel. This don't mean you and me is settled up.

Sutton

"What the hell you waitin' for, Jimmy?" Mannin Clements insisted.

Taylor didn't answer. He still wasn't convinced that Sutton wasn't out to set him up. Finally he lifted his gray hat and waved his men forward.

Taylor had forty armed men behind him as he came into the south end of DeWitt Street and passed Hallstetter's Livery Stable. A chorus of hoots and howls went up as they passed Maybell's. One of the girls was on the balcony jiggling her bare tits with her hands.

"Tell the men to spread out," Taylor said to Clements when he saw Sutton's men lining the streets at the north end of town. "And I don't want no shootin' unless they go first."

Taylor tied his paint up in front of the Gulf. He had the expression of a hawk and his eyes darted about like those of a barn owl hunting its prey. Clements traded nasty looks with the Sutton man perched on the freight wagon.

Taylor stopped at the opening to the dining room and fixed his eyes on the older Sutton. Tallman allowed that he'd never seen so much hatred pass without words from one man to another. He also had his eye on Garwood. Since Sutton's mention of the carpetbaggers, the banker had been fidgety. Carefully, Taylor took a seat opposite Sutton.

"Well, now," Garwood said quickly as soon as Taylor was seated. "As you know—"

"I'll take over, Garwood," Tallman said boldly as he stepped up to the table. "Mr. Gill. You mind coming over here?" Tallman commanded. "You, too, Sheriff Kelly."

"What the—" Garwood blurted. "This is—"

"Hold on to your britches, Garwood," Tallman said.

Gill walked over to the table and glared at the Baptist banker.

Tallman undid the button on his jacket with his right hand in case he had to get at his Colt in a hurry. Then he reached into his left jacket pocket for the note he'd found on Hayward. When he went in for the slip of paper, he felt two of Wagner's deadly little spheres.

Kelly moved up to the table and looked on with blank eyes.

"I found this note on Frank Hayward two nights ago when he and a hired thug tried to burn the Hawkins barn." He threw it on the table in front of Sutton. Sutton read it quickly and passed it to Taylor who eyed the paper carefully. All the while, Tallman stared at the Scotsman, looking for some reaction. Then something struck him. The fifteen one-hundred-dollar banknotes were Cuero Safe Deposit Company gold certificates.

He turned quickly toward Garwood. The banker's forehead was shiny with perspiration.

"My name is Ash Tallman," he said, breaking the silence, "not Henry Ravensdale. Now I know for a fact that Hayward tried to burn out Horace Taylor *and* June Hawkins. One Taylor. One Sutton. That doesn't make sense." He turned and glared at Garwood. "You know anything about that? Or maybe about Jake Hawkins? Pitkin Taylor? Doc Blanchard?"

All eyes fell on Garwood.

Then he jumped up and away from the table, a .32 vest gun in his hand. "So you're one of the Pinkertons," he groaned.

"You kill my daddy?" Jim Taylor shouted as he pushed his chair away from the table.

Garwood pointed the small revolver in Taylor's face.

That's when Vivian put the cold steel of her .41 derringer against the back of Garwood's skull. "And

I'm the other Pinkerton," she said, her voice ringing a dead serious note: "The wages of sin is death," she added.

"Kelly! You son of a bitch. Do something!" Garwood shouted at the sheriff. "I don't pay you all that money for nothing."

Before Garwood had finished, Kelly lifted his long Colt out of its leather and trained it on Tallman's stomach. The gutless lawman was scared to death. "Drop that gun, woman," he said, his hand shaking.

Taylor and Sutton sat dumbfounded. They'd realized how they'd been used.

Vivian set the small gun on the table. She saw Tallman going slowly into his left pocket.

Just as Garwood snatched Vivian's derringer off the table, Tallman fingered a grenade from his pocket and heaved it backward against the wall. Like the others, the little silver ball exploded in a shower of sparks, smoke and metal shards.

Undaunted by the chaos, Jim Taylor bolted upright in the smoke-filled room and thumbed three quick shots into Garwood's fancy white shirt. The banker fell in a heap as if his legs had been kicked out from under him. Then Taylor quickly pointed his gun at the crooked sheriff and spent his last two shells in the man's face. The shower of brain pulp and blood covered Vivian.

At once the town of Cuero sounded like the battle of Bull Run as the feudists in the street began firing on each other as they scrambled for cover.

Tallman grabbed Vivian's wrist and jerked her toward the hotel kitchen. He knew that the war was on for sure—a fight to the death. He dragged his partner through the kitchen and out the back door. After a quick look around, they ran for the shack which housed the hotel's steam-powered water pump.

It was only after he slammed the door on the flimsy wooden structure that he felt the sharp pain in his neck. He reached up and grabbed the spot. It was then that he felt the blood.

TWENTY-THREE

As the warmth of the morning sun crept across his bed, Tallman began to stir. Though the room at the Capital Hotel in Austin was as comfortable as any he'd stayed in, he hadn't had a restful night since his one evening in Lockhart, nearly a week before the confrontation at the Gulf Hotel.

He'd spent the best part of Monday night in the pumphouse with Vivian. After she had pried the piece of shrapnel from his neck with his pocketknife and stopped the bleeding, they had settled in to listen to the fireworks.

The rest of the week he'd been plagued by the painful gash in his neck. And it didn't help that Garwood had known that two Pinkertons were on the case. The governor's breach of security had nagged at him in a way that caused him more discomfort than his wound.

"Yeah," Tallman grumbled when he heard the knock on his door.

"It's me—Vivian."

Tallman padded to the door in his underdrawers and let his partner in.

She was cleaned up and decked out like she was headed for lunch with the Queen of England. Her mood was buoyant.

"Damn, Ash," she charged. "You gonna make it another day?"

Tallman managed a thin smile as he rubbed the sleep from his eyes. Then he felt his neck. The small dressing was damp again. "Do me a favor?" he groaned after a yawn. "Put some new gauze on this cut."

"Sure."

Vivian cleaned the wound which was just above his collar line and left for the dining room. "Put on a new face before you come downstairs to breakfast, partner," she said, teasing him as she left the room. "You surely don't want to be in a foul mood when you dine this afternoon with His Excellency, the Governor."

At noon a Texas Ranger arrived to take them to the statehouse for a one o'clock lunch with Trowbridge.

Austin was bustling under the hot September sun. The sky was partly obscured by clouds. The humidity was ninety-eight percent, and the streets were congested with well-groomed people and carriages from the statehouse.

Holt Lawry, their Ranger escort, ushered them into the elaborate governor's office. The beautiful mahogany paneling and the detailed trim work looked as if it had taken a hundred carpenters a hundred years.

"This here's Mr. Stockworth," Lawry said, introducing the tall and skinny assistant to the governor. "He'll take care of you."

"Thanks, Mr. Lawry," Vivian said to the ruddy Ranger.

Tallman nodded his thanks.

"I'll be in the hallway. Just holler when you want a ride back to the hotel."

"We'll do that, sir," Vivian said.

Tallman took a brief look at Stockworth, sucked the ash on his cigar to a red glow and then blew a cloud of smoke in his direction. He'd taken an instant dislike to the man.

"Have a seat," Stockworth said finally, somewhat unnerved by the detective's gaze and clouds of cigar smoke. "The governor is busy with an important matter."

The pair of Pinkertons sat quietly as the hands of the large, upright clock chimed at one. Then at one thirty.

When the clock chimed twice, signaling Tallman

that they'd been waiting for an hour, he got up and turned to Vivian. "Let's go," he said. "We'll get the four o'clock to New Orleans." Allan Pinkerton's last telegram had directed them to contact one of their agents there as John Wesley Hardin had been last seen in that city.

"Wait a minute!" Stockworth said as he got up from his massive desk. "You don't just get up and walk away from the governor of Texas."

Tallman walked slowly toward the hawk-faced assistant, his cigar wedged into his teeth. "That a fact?" he sneered at Stockworth as he grabbed a handful of jacket, shirt and bow tie, and twisted the cloth tight on the man's scrawny neck. "Well, looks like we just set a new rule of political protocol."

"Ash! Let's go," Vivian insisted as she put her hand on his shoulder. "This is hardly worth working up a sweat over."

"You tell Trowbridge that we'll be back with Hardin just like we're gettin' paid to do," he growled as he twisted the man's collar tighter and blew more cigar smoke. "And you tell him I'm going to find out how Sheridan Garwood learned that there were Pinkerton agents in Cuero. If he had anything to do with it, he'll answer to me."

Then he threw the white-faced man into his leather chair and stomped from the elaborate waiting room. Vivian trailed along.

"Need a ride, sir?" Holt Lawry asked as Tallman strode by, trailing cigar smoke.

"Thanks," Vivian said, looking back. "But I guess we'll walk."

TWENTY-FOUR

The muggy coastal heat hung over Pensacola like a wet sheet. The six-wheel Prescott Flyer locomotive hissed, squealed and lurched as it came to a stop in the busy station.

Tallman was looking forward to steady ground after two days and two nights on the shuddering train. Though the accommodations had been the best money could buy, he could only take so much railroading.

When they had arrived in New Orleans, they'd received an envelope from the stationmaster. Ed Duncan, the Pinkerton charged with the capture of John Wesley Hardin, had informed him that the outlaw had been seen in Pensacola and that he was going on to the panhandle city. Once they'd read the note, they didn't bother to get off. The train was bound for Biloxi, Mobile and Pensacola.

As the conductor walked the narrow passageway chanting Pennn-saah-coal-ah, Tallman grabbed his bag and left his tiny sleeper.

"Viv," he shouted at the closed door of the adjoining compartment.

"No need to shout, Ash," she said as she appeared in the narrow doorway with a sensuous smile. She had on a teal blue dress trimmed with sparkling white embroidery. Her auburn hair was clean and curled and a thin gold necklace accented her ample cleavage.

"That doesn't look like an outlaw-huntin' getup," he kidded her.

"You like?"

"No man could resist."

Once on the platform amidst teary-eyed friends and relatives of the new arrivals, Tallman scanned the area for a redcap.

"Tallman and Valentine?" a soothing voice asked from behind.

"Yeah," Tallman replied as he turned to face the young man.

"Ed Duncan."

"Pleased to meet you, Duncan. Heard a lot about you," he said honestly. Though the man was just over twenty, he'd already built a reputation as one of Pinkerton's better agents, when it came to particularly nasty assignments. It was rumored that he had been orphaned at age twelve and had fended for himself on San Francisco's waterfront until one of the older agents recruited him for a job two years earlier.

Then Vivian noticed the man next to Duncan. When her eyes met his, he introduced himself. "John Armstrong, ma'am. Texas Rangers." Then he turned to Tallman. "Mr. Tallman. My pleasure."

"I know you by reputation, Lieutenant," Tallman said as he tipped his flat-brim Stetson ever so slightly. Armstrong was one of the top dogs in the outfit. "Well, what say we all find a place to have a cool one? Big city like this ought to have ice."

Vivian agreed, noticing that the crispness had already vanished from her dress and that her curls were stretching in the still, humid air. "You can give us the lowdown on Hardin."

"Here, Miss Valentine," Duncan said, taking her bag with one hand and her arm with the other. "I know just the place."

"Lead the way," Tallman said.

"Looks like you'll be able to enjoy a nice meal this evening, get a good night's rest, and join us tomorrow on a train ride to Austin." The Texas Ranger had a smile a yard wide and an easygoing voice.

"Hardin?"

"Restin' up in the Pensacola jailhouse. Paperwork's even done."

Tallman's shoulders sagged at the thought of another two days on the rails. But he wasn't disturbed by the news that Hardin was behind bars. He'd had enough of the Suttons and the Taylors and anything related. He was ready to move on.

"Heard from the chief about what we're to do?" Tallman asked Duncan.

"Nope. Last word I had was that you two were to help stand guard on Hardin while we drag him back to Austin," he said after turning and walking backward for several steps.

Tallman swung his feet to the oak flooring in his compact sleeper. He'd been awakened by the groaning deceleration of the train. Just as the breeze sent a hearty whiff of coal smoke into his open window, he saw a small station go by slowly. Then the milk-run special jolted to a stop. He looked at his pocket watch, which was next to his Colt New Line on the small night table. It was six fifteen. He rubbed his eyes and looked back at the unpainted wood frame station. A small sign over the door read: LACOMBE, LOUISIANA. In the distance he could see the morning sun shimmering off Lake Pontchartrain.

With his mind drifting toward a steaming cup of coffee, he washed up in the china basin and dressed in his beige Henry Ravensdale suit, taking particular care with his cross-draw rig and his forearm derringer. He dropped two more Wagner impact grenades into his jacket pocket.

Having pitched the bowler he'd used in the writer disguise, he gladly seated his favorite flat-brim Stetson and went to Armstrong's sleeper.

He found the elder Texas Ranger up, dressed, and enjoying one of his roll-your-owns. "How about some eggs and sausage, John? Before we take over for Vivian and the kid?"

"Lead the way, Ash," Armstrong said as he popped off the seat. "Got a mind to hear some more of them war stories of yours."

Before they'd pulled out of Pensacola with John Wesley Hardin, they had decided that they'd take up an eight-hour watch system, with two people on Hardin at all times. Since Ed Duncan and Vivian had seemed to hit it off during their single night in Pensacola, Tallman had suggested at dinner that evening that he and Armstrong make one team and that Duncan and Vivian comprise the other.

When he'd seen Ed Duncan and Vivian emerge from her hotel room early the next morning, he knew he'd made a wise decision. Vivian was grinning like a little girl on her first date to a church social, while Duncan had a sheepish look on his face and he appeared dog tired. Tallman had chuckled inwardly and couldn't help think that the blond-headed lad had experienced a woman as he'd never done before.

After they'd settled in the day before, Armstrong and Tallman had taken the first watch at four P.M. They had immediately hit it off and had taken pleasure in trading war stories and a moderate amount of Tallman's favorite brand of Kentucky sour mash, Stillman's Gold.

They had just started out to the far end of the car when the train lurched forward and nearly knocked them off their feet.

"Jesus Christ!" Armstrong muttered. "The son of a bitch who drives this machine must beat his wife and kids."

Tallman chortled as he grabbed a door frame to steady himself. Armstrong was one of those people who could bring a man to laughter by the *way* he said something rather than by what he said.

"How's things?" Tallman asked as they stopped by the compartment.

Hardin didn't look around.

"We'll be ready for *you* at eight," Vivian groaned. "Makes for a long night."

"See you in a bit," Tallman said as he led the way to the dining car.

Armstrong tipped his large, black Stetson Canadian as he went by Vivian.

They'd leased all six sleepers on the car so that

they'd not have to be bothered by rubberneckers or anyone else. And the Texas Southern Railway had been kind enough to put them directly behind the coal tender. It was a long walk to the dining car, which was in front of the caboose, but they were isolated.

Armstrong ordered four scrambled eggs and a stack of pancakes. After a better than average breakfast and several cups of strong coffee, Armstrong got going on Hardin.

"I detect a sympathetic note," Tallman added after the tall, square-shouldered Ranger had sketched Hardin's past.

"Let's say I think I understand. One man's sense of justice don't always mesh with another man's picture of what's right and wrong. When them boys in Concord, Massachusetts, loaded up them redcoats with lead balls, I don't imagine they felt none like cold-blooded killers. More likely they fancied themselves heroes."

Tallman nodded and took a cheroot from his vest pocket.

"Now the way I figure it, Hardin's felt that every man he's sent to boot hill deserved the trip. He don't seem to me to be some sort of madman killer."

Armstrong then ran his fingers through his thick salt-and-pepper hair and stretched as if to signal the end of his talk on Hardin.

The waiter approached and began to clear the table.

Armstrong got out his Bulldog tobacco and a package of papers and started to roll one of his wrinkled cigarettes.

"Of course I know a couple of Pinkertons who'd argue with you," Tallman said.

Armstrong grunted something and fired up the end of his smoke. "Way I heard it, the one called Buck went for Hardin like an Apache hopped up on loco weed, hollerin', waving his hogleg. Hardin just done what come natural. He had a mind to save his hide; so he shot 'em dead."

Tallman smiled at Armstrong's analysis. Knowing Buck Kingsford as he did, he didn't doubt the story.

At a quarter to eight, they started back to the sleeper car to relieve Vivian and Duncan. At the end of the dining car, Tallman saw a pile of morning newspapers and a water glass of coins. A small headline had caught his eye: TROWBRIDGE ISSUES MURDER WARRANTS. He fished four pennies from his pocket, dropped them in the glass, took a paper, and followed the old Ranger back to the car.

As soon as Vivian and Duncan had been relieved, they headed for her room.

"Guess they ain't hungry, Ash." Armstrong chortled. "Leastwise not for bacon and eggs."

"Doesn't seem like it."

Armstrong pulled hard on his roll-your-own and held a thin smile as he exhaled a stream of Bulldog smoke. "That reminds me, Ash. I ain't told you yet that I found out why God made women."

"Why's that, John?" Tallman said, playing straight man to another of the Ranger's jokes.

"God couldn't teach sheep how to cook."

Hardin laughed harder than they did when he heard the line through the two open doors. They had the shades up on the passageway windows and the doors open so they could keep a clear watch on their prisoner.

After a few more women jokes, Armstrong settled back and watched the scenery flash by. Tallman got his paper off the seat and went to the headline. Though he'd calmed down over the leak at the governor's office and the run-in with the pipsqueak secretary, Stockworth, the anger hadn't disappeared completely.

The article in the *New Orleans Morning Journal* claimed that murder warrants had been issued by the state of Texas for Jim Taylor, Bill Sutton, Mannin Clements, Lefty Walters and many of the others. Confirming the other newspaper stories he'd seen in Austin before leaving for Florida, the *Journal* claimed that twenty-two men were killed in the two-day shoot-out which had ensued at the Gulf Hotel after the shooting deaths of Sheridan Garwood and Pete Kelly. Tallman had heard that the Gulf Hotel gunfight had made all the papers in the East. By the size of the *New Orleans Morning Journal* article, he didn't doubt that the DeWitt County battle had become a national incident. He read on with great interest. "Be damned," he muttered to himself when he saw Gill's name. He read on:

Nathan Gill, a prominent Cuero real estate man, has made a handsome offer to the Estate of Sheridan Garwood for Garwood's stock in the Cuero Safe Deposit Company.

The troubled bank has been closed since the incident due to cash flow problems. The executors of the Garwood Estate have repossessed three of the four largest ranches in DeWitt County. Only June Hawkins's JJ Ranch remains clear. To the surprise of estate executors, she made her back payments at the bank, cleared all of her accounts in town, paid back wages to her hands, and financed a lavish funeral for Pop Mead, a family friend who'd been killed in the feuding.

Tallman smiled. He'd seen to it that the fifteen hundred dollars in Hayward's wallet found its way to her.

"Gill has also tendered cash offers on the three repossessed ranches of Bill Sutton, Jim Taylor and Horace Taylor," Tallman read on. "The executors are expected to agree to Gill's terms in order to restore bank solvency."

"Looks interestin'," Armstrong grunted when he noticed Tallman's intensity.

"Oh, nothing really. Just the goin's-on over in De-Witt County. There's a runt of a Scot who's about to own the county by the looks of it."

"Nate Gill?" Armstrong asked.

"You know him?"

"Nope. Just about him. Governor hates his ass somethin' fierce."

"Well I guess he's buyin' up the Taylors' and Bill Sutton's spreads as well as the controlling interest in the Cuero bank."

"No doubt," Armstrong added as he blew a stream of smoke. "He's frontin' for a syndicate of Scotch whiskey merchants in New York. He'll have all the money he needs. Ain't never been nobody in the whiskey business who's shy of money."

"Damn, too bad we didn't talk sooner. You seem to know more about the feuding than anyone I've talked to yet."

"Know mostly about Gill. Governor set me on him to learn what I could. Gill was backin' a good old Rebel Democrat for governor. Trowbridge took it personal." He paused and then grunted: "Pola-ticks!"

"Guess you get your fill of it, being a top-dog Ranger in Austin?" Tallman asked.

Armstrong grunted and nodded slowly. His eyes

told the story. He'd likely prefer eating horse apples or playing with rattlesnakes over politics.

Tallman laughed, recalling his walking out on the governor. "Guess I'll be in hot water with your governor," Tallman went on. "Friday past, I nearly killed that son of a bitch Stockworth and I walked out on the chief of state after he'd kept us waiting an hour."

"Goddamn, Ash! Mebbe you'd ought to get off at the border. He'll likely have a hundred of my men out after you," Armstrong kidded. "You don't never say no to His Excellency."

Tallman wedged a fresh cheroot into his teeth and gave the likable Ranger a broad smile.

"Standin' up the king is a worse crime than roughin' up that jackass Gilbert Stockworth," Armstrong added as he twirled the end of his handlebar mustache.

"He's some piece of work," Tallman added as the train began to brake for another small town.

"Him and that banker that died and went to Heaven were always huddled together up in the statehouse."

"Garwood?" Tallman said as he bolted upright.

"Some of us even wondered if they was sweet on each other!" Armstrong belted out a real horselaugh. But then he cut it off when he saw that Tallman didn't find it amusing.

TWENTY-FIVE

Tallman stormed into the governor's outer office and literally pulled Gilbert Stockworth over his elaborate mahogany desk. Papers scattered, the inkwell slopped onto the carpet, and a collection of desktop knickknacks flew in every direction.

Armstrong tried hard to keep a straight face as Tallman dragged the gagging assistant into Trowbridge's palatial office. He was sitting with three very dignified characters. All were stunned at the cyclonic entrance.

"Armstrong!" the governor shouted. "What the hell is going on here?"

The three visitors bolted upright and their faces went pale.

"Armstrong! Arrest this man!" he shouted, pointing toward Tallman. "Her, too," he added when Vivian came through the door.

"Mr. Tallman has a problem," Armstrong said quietly.

"Now see here—"

"Shut up!" Tallman growled at the overweight politician. "And listen!" He released his grip on Stockworth's collar enough so that the assistant could breathe. "You lost two of your best Rangers. I'm convinced you have a Judas here and I'm further convinced that I'm holding him by his skinny neck right now. Garwood knew there were two Pinkertons in Cuero."

"We thought on it most of the way back on the train, Governor. All seems to fit together," Armstrong added. "Nothing else adds up."

The governor's face became white and Tallman was looking carefully into his eyes for any sign of complicity.

Stockworth suddenly shrieked like a gut-shot coyote and pulled away. He had a .25-caliber five-shot Hopkins revolver in his hand. For a moment he had a pleading look on his face as he turned toward the governor. Then without warning he began firing.

Everyone was too stunned to react. Everyone but Armstrong. The Texas Ranger slowly pulled his long-barrel Colt .45 and shot Stockworth in the head before the Judas had time to pull the vest gun trigger for the fourth time. The skinny man's head erupted in a mist of red pulp as the room thundered with the single shot. Though a third of his skull was gone, the governor's secretary appeared to spin and jump for several moments as if he was doing some sort of offbeat jig. Then, as quick as a flash of lightning, the macabre dance ended. Stockworth fell over as if blown down by a stick of dynamite.

Tallman looked over at Armstrong. He showed no visible emotion as he holstered the smoking Colt. He could have been shooting an empty whiskey bottle off a fence post.

"I'm shot. I'm shot," one of the governor's visitors cried.

Tallman looked over and saw blood on the man's thigh. He went over and put his finger in the small hole in the man's pants and ripped them open. The small bullet had only creased the man's leg. And the man had peed his pants.

"You'll live, mister," Tallman grunted.

Suddenly the governor was shouting again. "Armstrong! Arrest these people!"

"What people?" he asked calmly.

"Him!" he pointed to Tallman. "Her!" He pointed again.

"Far as I know they ain't broke no laws," Armstrong added.

Then a small chair jumped. Everyone turned toward the ghostly occurrence. Stockworth's body lurched again and went limp. A puddle of urine crept from under the corpse.

Tallman walked toward Trowbridge and put his face close to the politician's mug. "I didn't like what I saw in your eyes when Stockworth broke away. You hear me, mister? Something tells me you were in on this. And if I ever hear of any proof, you and me will see each other again. Alone!"

People began pouring into the office.

"Armstrong! I'm ordering you for the last time," Trowbridge shouted as Tallman and Vivian headed for the door. "You—"

"You tub of horseshit," Armstrong said with a sigh. "Arrest them yourself."

"You're fired!"

"No I ain't. I quit."

TWENTY-SIX

Ed Duncan, John Armstrong, Vivian and Tallman were having a howling good time at one of Austin's wildest eateries. A four-piece band, two banjos, a piano and an upright bass, hammered out lively tunes while the patrons ate chicken, ribs, corn on the cob and popcorn, and drank cold beer. Though the tablecloths were paper, the tables were bench-type rigs, the beer mugs were cheap, and the floor was covered with sawdust, Pete's Rib Joint had class.

At midnight, Armstrong claimed that he needed some shut-eye. He was planning to set out later in the week for Flagstaff, a growing town in the Arizona Territory. He'd claimed that he'd had many offers to sheriff towns further west. Flagstaff was one of the most recent proposals.

"Keep a lookout over your shoulder, John," Tallman insisted as he stood up with the square-shouldered lawdog.

"I'll do that, Ash. And I'll stay in touch with some of the boys in Austin. If we get anything certain on that shit-bird, Trowbridge, you'll be the first to know." Then the ex-Ranger seated his large black Stetson, nodded, touched the brim as a so-long gesture, and walked off.

Tallman felt bad. He knew the man had been a proud Ranger. But he also knew that Flagstaff would be getting a hell of a lawman.

"Good man," Vivian said when she saw his pensive expression.

They had another round of cold draughts, but the cheer had faded and the conversation began to wane.

"We leaving for Gray Bull in the morning?" Vivian asked after he was out of earshot.

"We don't have to be there until the twenty-first," Tallman said. "That's eight days."

Pinkerton had wired them at the Capitol Hotel that they were to meet Robert O. Coulp, III, an investigator for the House Committee on Indian Affairs. The agency had been retained to get to the bottom of theft, murder and conspiracy on the Wind River Indian Reservation, which lay outside of Gray Bull, Wyoming.

"Be honest with you, Viv," he lied. "I want to take a day or two to nose around Cuero. I'd still like to nail Trowbridge's carcass to the barn door."

Vivian beamed a devilish smile. She knew he was going to do some snooping around, but she also knew it had nothing to do with Governor Trowbridge. He was headed straight to June Hawkins's ranch and the only snooping he'd be doing would be in the widow's underdrawers.

And Tallman knew that she knew.

"What say we meet in Denver at the Spencer?" Tallman suggested. "Four days from now. That will give us a couple of days and three nights before we have to leave for Gray Bull."

"Now that's one of the better ideas you've had lately," she noted with a gleam of anticipation in her eyes. The Spencer was Denver's finest hotel. "We surely need a rest."

"Figure we'll get any rest?" he teased as he backed his chair away from the table and stood up.

"Ash, you'll surely need some after a couple of days with June Hawkins," she added, her knowing eyes flashing in the yellow lantern light.

Tallman pulled an expensive cheroot from his vest pocket, put a flaming match to the cigar, and took two steps toward the door before turning around. He touched the brim of his hat and said, "See you in Denver."

"You can bet on it, Ash."

Tallman grinned. "I already have."